Dad's Army

A CELEBRATION

RICHARD WEBBER

Virgin

ACKNOWLEDGEMENTS

It's only when the final words have been written and there is time to reflect that you realise just how many people help in the creation of such a book. I would like to thank the staff at Spotlight, Equity and in particular Amanda at BBC's Artists' Index for supplying numerous contact numbers. Thanks are also due to BBC Written Archives for permission to publish Paul Fox and Michael Mills' memos. The BBC has also kindly allowed me to use a number of their photographs.

I am indebted to the photographic skills of David Porter, and to all the cast members, as well as friends and family of deceased cast members, who kindly allowed the use of their photos to help illustrate the book. Also thanks to everyone who gave up their time to speak with me about the series.

As always, Hilary Johnson's guidance and advice have been of great help. And Jack Wheeler, of the Dad's Army Appreciation Society, has played an important role in making sure I avoid any factual slip-ups during what has been a hectic research period – thank you for your time.

Rod Green and Hal Norman at Virgin have been enthusiastic about the project from the start. And it's an honour to have Michael Palin, who's a fan of the programme himself, writing a foreword for the book. I'm grateful to them all.

This project would not have been possible but for Jimmy Perry and David Croft's support. I would like to thank them for allowing me the opportunity to write a book about their masterpiece, and for giving up so much of their time to talk with me about the show.

Finally, I would once again like to thank Paula for her support during what has been an extremely busy period of my life.

This book is dedicated to my father and late mother, with all my love.

First published in 1997 by
Virgin Books
an imprint of Virgin Publishing Ltd
332 Ladbroke Grove
London W10 5AH

A catalogue record for this book is available from the British Library.

ISBN 1-85227-694-0

Designed by Design 23, London
Printed and bound in Great Britain by Butler & Tanner Ltd, Frome and London

CONTENTS

FOREWORD

In the summer of 1969, when we were preparing the first Monty Python series, the BBC Light Entertainment wardrobe department had begun more and more to resemble an army barracks. It was almost impossible to find a decent dress or a Spanish cardinal's cloak, but if it was air-raid warden's helmets or bicycle clips you wanted, you'd come to the right place. The culprit was *Dad's Army*, a series about the Home Guard that, despite some adverse initial reactions, had been given the go-ahead for a second series. From then on it never looked back, and its triumph over initial uncertainty gave much hope to us, when, later that year, the first Monty Python show was broadcast to a resounding silence.

Dad's Army succeeded for all the right reasons. The authors, Jimmy Perry and David Croft, knew their ground and created their characters with precision, affection and confidence. Rarely has there been a television comedy series with so many good parts for all the cast. Though everyone had their individual favourites (I adored John Le Mesurier's desperately pained counterpoint to Arthur Lowe), it was a triumph of ensemble acting, and writing so surefooted that the time came when certain characters hardly needed to say anything. They merely had to be in the frame for the laughter to start.

Dad's Army gave me the same sort of pleasure as the *Just William* books. It was a very British pleasure, relying on sly wit and subversiveness served up in a convincing, appealing, meticulously well-observed world. It was a world which though it remained always a little fresh and innocent, contained within it so many truths about human behaviour that all of us could see something of someone we knew in each episode. The universal truths in *Dad's Army* were surely the reason for its extraordinary and enduring appeal. It was never a vehicle for a wisecracking star. It did not strain to bludgeon or dazzle with its humour. It was accessible and humane and touching and irresistibly funny because it was true.

Jimmy Perry and David Croft have created one of the most endearing of all comedy classics. Their glorious cast has marched into television immortality. No success could give me more pleasure, and I am sure that I shall be only one of many who will pore over this rich and definitive book, full of gems of information about the making of the series. Richard Webber has marshalled facts and figures and firsthand memories into an indispensable manual to life in and around Walmington Church Hall. A life which will never be forgotten.

Michael Palin, London, 1997

Introduction

In 1973, the *Dad's Army* team was invited to switch on the Blackpool illuminations. After a lot of cajoling and subtle threats they all agreed to do it.

It had been arranged for us to be picked up at Preston and driven into Blackpool by road. The train pulled into Preston station where three large Rolls Royce cars were waiting for us.

Then came the problem. Who was going to sit with whom, and who was going to ride in the leading car? John Laurie pointed at Arnold Ridley (who

was only a year older than him), and said, 'I'm not riding in the same car as that silly old fool and I'm going to sit in the front one. It's my right. I'm the only proper actor here.'

We reached Blackpool, where the heavens opened up and the rain poured down. We were due to switch on the Illuminations at 10pm from a balcony outside the Town Hall, and as zero hour approached we discussed the situation. We couldn't keep the crowds waiting and the rain was still tipping down.

Suddenly Arthur Lowe disappeared and in his place stood Captain Mainwaring. He turned to us and said 'We're not going to let a little rain stop us, are we? Come on men!' We trooped out onto the balcony to be greeted with a roar by the thousands of umbrellas and raincoated figures below. Arthur turned on the lights, and the rain promptly stopped.

The *Dad's Army* team became the characters they portrayed, and the characters became them. They were a bunch of tough old pros, and during the nine years we were together there was virtually no unpleasantness. Perhaps the occasional muttering and a hostile glare or two, but then no-one's perfect.

Sadly most of the cast never lived long enough to see themselves become legends. If they had, John Laurie would be 100 and Arnold Ridley 101.

Jimmy Perry, London, 1997

We used to call them 'the magnificent seven'. Once or twice a year they would assemble at Thetford ready for filming. On the first morning Arthur Lowe would arrive on the location a few minutes late. This was partly due to the fact that he was, after all, the captain and therefore should be last on parade, and not a little due to the unusually delicate nature of his constitution.

John Le Mesurier was always on time. This was just as well because all his buttons would be undone and his webbing equipment twisted. The wardrobe department would have to labour to restore some sort of order to the general shambles which they came to know and love as well.

Clive Dunn's greeting was usually 'What are we doing?' which infuriated my assistants who had spent hours producing a comprehensive schedule which nobody ever read.

John Laurie would have completed most of *The Times* crossword. He would glance surreptitiously at Ian Lavender's empty squares and say with triumph 'Whisht . . . what's the matter with your brains, lad?' His beady eye would then fall on Arnold Ridley who would be bravely limping into make-up. 'Poor old boy . . . look at him, he's falling apart.

Usually last would come Jimmy Beck, looking the worse for wear having stayed up until the early hours talking to John Le Mesurier. John never appeared to need sleep.

And then we would go to work. It was a hard day for some elderly gentlemen and if anyone had told them that they were taking a leading part in a golden age of comedy they would have said 'Pull the other one'. But they were all gold – 22 carat. And it was fun – wonderful fun!

David Croft, Suffolk, 1997

The History of Dad's Army

On the eve of its 30th anniversary, *Dad's Army* is still the undisputed doyen in the pantheon of British comedy. Few, if any, programmes attract continual prime time transmissions so long after first gracing our screens. With audience figures regularly trouncing that of its rivals, one can only sit back and admire gleefully this pearl of a programme penned by Jimmy Perry and David Croft.

Often TV classics mature with age and this is true to some extent of Dad's Army. Critics and audiences weren't bowled over by the escapades of an ensemble of mainly veteran character actors when the first series was aired in 1968. But that was soon to change.

Today, it continues to pull in large audiences whenever an episode is screened, and what is promising as far as its longevity is concerned is its pulling power with a younger audience as well as the hardened fans. Astonishingly, some of its fans haven't even graduated from infant school, ensuring that *Dad's Army*

Arthur Lowe as Captain Mainwaring.

will still be a favourite well into the new millennium.

When the idea for a show about the Home Guard was conceived, Jimmy Perry was working for Joan Littlewood at the Theatre Royal in the East London suburb of Stratford.

At this point in his career, Jimmy's only experience in the medium of TV was as an actor; his writing output consisted of pantomimes and comedy sketches. But for some time he'd harboured a desire to write for the small screen. 'I kept telling myself that I must write for TV because I could create a good part for myself – that was the main reason for writing *Dad's Army*,' laughs Jimmy.

On his daily train ride to Stratford East, he considered the idea. He was convinced of one thing: the success of *Bilko* and *The Army Game* proved that a good service comedy series never failed. 'It was important I wrote about something I'd experienced and understood; then I thought about the Home Guard. After all, I'd served in it at Barnes and Watford during the Second World War.

'It seemed a wonderful subject for

comedy – and one that hadn't been tackled before.' But it was 1967, over 20 years since the war had finished, and no one mentioned the Home Guard anymore.

Jimmy acknowledged ruefully that everyone had forgotten about the role the Home Guard played during the war, and that included the librarian at his local public library. 'I went along to see what books they had on the subject and was astonished when the librarian asked: "The Home Guard, what's that then?"'

Next stop on his research trail was the Imperial War Museum. After returning home with pamphlets describing how to make Molotov cocktails, the memories

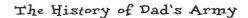
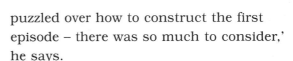

Edward Sinclair and Bill Pertwee provide the bookends.

puzzled over how to construct the first episode – there was so much to consider,' he says.

He gained his much-needed inspiration from the Will Hay movie, *Oh! Mr Porter,* which was being screened that Sunday afternoon. 'One of the movie's strengths was the wonderful balance of characters: a pompous man, a boy and an old man. The combination made for perfect comedy.' This was a key influence when writing his first script, *The Fighting Tigers.*

Switch on any episode of *Dad's Army* and one laughs at the almost crazy antics Captain Mainwaring and his ill-equipped, ill-trained platoon get up to; but all the time Jimmy Perry and David Croft were drawing on their own wartime experiences when scripting the memorable series.

The dearth of weapons at the beginning of the series, the makeshift alternatives comprising of golf clubs, old shotguns and other oddities were all reflections of what life was like for Jimmy in the real Home Guard. 'One section of the first episode considers how to tackle a tank with a burning blanket – I remember having lectures about that,' he says.

When the first script was completed, he was chuffed with the result. But he put it aside for several weeks and continued with his work at Joan Littlewood's Theatre Workshop.

came flooding back. 'I was a 15-year-old boy in the Home Guard, and it was an exciting time. I was convinced this was a subject that could be successfully explored through comedy.'

Jimmy set to work. He sketched out a brief synopsis, gave some thought to the principal characters and settled down to write the first script. 'For a while I

During the summer of 1967, while the theatre was taking a two-month break, Jimmy's then agent, who also happened to be David Croft's wife, rang offering him a small part in *Beggar My Neighbour*, which David was directing for the BBC.

Playing Reg Varney's uncouth brother, led to an opportunity Jimmy wasn't going to miss. 'We were rehearsing at a boys' club on a hot summer's day. I saw David fiddling about with his white sports car and grasped the opportunity to tell him about my script. He was non-committal but agreed to read it.'

The following Monday was the day of recording. As the hours ticked by, Jimmy began fearing the worst until David approached him enthused by the idea. Once a second script had been written, David Croft showed the idea to Michael Mills, then BBC's Head of Light Entertainment.

Mills shared Croft's avidity but wasn't convinced about the title *The Fighting Tigers*; it was his masterstroke that saw the programme renamed *Dad's Army*. On the proviso that David worked with Jimmy, taking into account his

Wilson's new uniform riled Mainwaring.

experience as a TV writer, on the scripts, Michael Mills was keen to proceed.

From the beginning, Jimmy and David's writing styles complemented each other. After getting together and roughing out detailed plots for two episodes, discussing the odd joke or piece of dialogue, they would go their separate ways and each write an episode. In all the years they scripted *Dad's Army*, they never felt the need to swap scripts and read one another's work. 'It was extraordinary how our writing styles were so similar,' says David. 'Whenever I watch an episode now, I can't tell who wrote it.'

Within six weeks of the day Jimmy passed his script to David, the BBC hierarchy had given the green light for six episodes to be made; but not before some concerns had been voiced. 'Nearly everyone involved was enthusiastic,' says Jimmy, 'and any opposition came from people worried about whether we were sending up the efforts of the Home Guard.'

The programme's format was battled over for some time before it was cleared for transmission. 'The original closing credits, for which I fought very hard, showed vignettes of the artists against a background of authentic war scenes,' explains David Croft.

Enormous phalanxes of marching troops contrasted the might of the German army with its tanks and guns against what Michael Mills described as the 'pathetic, comic, but valorous nature of the Home Guard.'

John Laurie was a master of facial expressions.

We also had shots of refugees in the opening credits but Paul Fox, BBC1's Controller at the time, was against it,' says David. 'I fought hard to keep the credits the way they were and remember

Arnold Ridley in chivalrous mode.

attending a meeting with Paul, Bill Cotton and Tom Sloan. Paul, realising how strongly I felt about the matter, finally agreed to the format I wanted. But having fought for so long, Tom Sloan suddenly decided that if Paul wasn't happy the credits should be changed.'

Sir Paul Fox believed the credits were not apposite for the type of programme being made. 'The shots I was unhappy about showed refugees and Nazi troops,

and to me they had absolutely nothing to do with the subject of the series, that was my concern.'

'Paul was also very worried about whether the show was taking the mickey out of Britain's Finest Hour,' David explains. 'For a while *Dad's Army* was on the verge of not going ahead. Then someone suggested having a prologue before the credits on the first episode showing the cast in the present day supporting the "I'm Backing Britain" campaign.

'So that's what happened but it meant the first episode appeared to start three times: first you had the prologue, then the familiar swastika and Union Jack credits and also the newsreel-style clippings before the show finally started. It was like a dog's dinner in my view, but that was the compromise that got the show on the air.'

With six episodes finally commissioned, David and Jimmy set about refining the main characters. One of the first to receive their attention was Frazer. 'We knew we had to have a Scotsman in the

Captain Mainwaring brings good news.

programme,' says Jimmy. 'In those days, every English southern town seemed to have a Scot who was always treated with great reverence by the English, although they were inclined to be a bit disdainful of the English people around them.' From this generalisation, the character of Frazer was born.

Next came the spiv. 'Everybody did a spiv, it was a common wartime character. Forty years ago, spivs traded out of suitcases all along London's Oxford Street, and whenever things were scarce, like during the war, you could guarantee there would be a spiv around.'

As for Jones, the ageing war veteran, Jimmy Perry delved into his Home Guard memories. With him then was an old soldier who'd seen action at the Battle of Omdurman in 1898. 'He was a lance

corporal, probably in his late sixties, and kept telling me about his war experiences with Kitchener against the Fuzzy Wuzzies. When it came to writing the series, I dug all these memories up and created Jones. As for the catchphrase "They don't like it up 'em", that came from a sergeant who taught me bayonet drill at Colchester barracks when I was called up in the regular army in 1944.

'Private Godfrey meanwhile dated from an era long gone when shop assistants politely asked whether you were being attended to, or if they could help,' says Jimmy. 'They loved their work and took great pride in serving customers. We needed a gentle character and Godfrey evolved.'

A vicar was required to be in charge of the church hall, the use of which was constantly argued over by Mainwaring and Hodges. The verger, so brilliantly portrayed by Edward Sinclair, started out as a caretaker and didn't don clerical attire until episode 16, *The Bullet Is Not For Firing*.

Frank Pike, the baby of the platoon, who's constantly mollycoddled by his mother, was based on Jimmy's experiences as a boy, while the character of Hodges explored an area of society that interests Jimmy. 'I've always been obsessed with people who never had a hope in hell of doing anything more than shuffling along in life, suddenly getting power.

'The warden has the power to fine people for showing a light. In *Dad's Army* we wanted someone to upset the pompous, middle-class Mainwaring, and

Hodges was certainly an irritant. In my experience, air raid wardens were often jumped up people from minor positions who exploited the power given to them by their duties.

'Hodges was certainly jumped up, something Mainwaring blamed on the fact that he was only a greengrocer – which incidentally generated lots of mail from

real life greengrocers!'

Once the characters had been agreed, Jimmy Perry and David Croft turned their minds to the difficult task of casting, a crucial component in any successful show. Jimmy had already given the matter some thought, recording his views on the original script of *The Fighting Tigers*.

It's hard to imagine anyone other than Messrs Lowe, Le Mesurier, Laurie *et al* playing the roles, but Jimmy initially saw

Mainwaring shows less fear than his troops.

Arthur Lowe playing Sergeant Wilson and Robert Dorning, who later appeared as a bank inspector in the episode *Something Nasty In The Vault*, as Captain Mainwaring. Jack Haig, meanwhile,

would play two characters: Jack Jones the butcher, although Jimmy had originally considered making him an ironmonger, and his twin brother, George.

Most of the cast were undefined at this early stage, but Jimmy wanted comic actor Arthur English to play Joe Walker, even though he had originally wanted to play the part himself. 'I wrote Walker for myself, but Michael Mills and David didn't think it was a good idea. Sadly, I was in no position to argue.'

Jimmy was disappointed not to be acting in the series he had created, but in hindsight believes it was probably for the best, a view echoed by David Croft. 'I realised Jimmy was disappointed not to be playing the spiv, but I feel authors are needed in the production box to see how things are going, and if they're also acting that's difficult.'

As he possessed little power in those days, Jimmy was grateful to David Croft for allowing him the chance to become involved in discussions regarding casting. 'I claim credit for Arthur Lowe,' he states. 'I kept telling David he should be in the show but the BBC weren't convinced, particularly Michael Mills. I remember him saying: "Arthur Lowe? We don't know him at the BBC, he doesn't work for us."'

Lowe was a big success as Mr Swindley in *Coronation Street*, but that was a Granada production. He was an actor whose reputation had been established primarily in commercial TV, and that didn't appeal to the BBC.

The part was first offered to actor Thorley Walters, and when he declined Jon Pertwee was considered. He also turned it down. Then, much to Jimmy's delight, Arthur Lowe was invited to meet Michael Mills, David and Jimmy at the BBC.

'One of the things I remember most about the meeting was Arthur putting his foot in it,' smiles Jimmy. 'We were sitting in the restaurant at Broadcasting House when Arthur said to David: "I'm not too fond of situation comedy, you know, I don't like the audience. One series I can't stand is that dreadful *Hugh and I*." David replied: "I produced it!" I couldn't believe how quickly Arthur changed his tack.'

After lengthy discussions, the part was finally offered to Arthur Lowe. He swiftly stamped his inimitable style on the character of Mainwaring, proving he was perfect for the part. But David Croft was unconvinced initially.

'We were taking a risk,' he admits. 'I knew him as Mr Swindley and he was very good, but the character was quite different from Mainwaring. I needn't have worried though because he slotted in to the role perfectly. The electricity between him and Wilson was wonderful.'

One of the challenges David faced when working with Arthur was getting him to learn his lines. 'He wouldn't take his script home and occasionally some of the other actors would call me at home insisting I get Arthur to learn the lines.

'So I started sending two copies of the

John Laurie and John Le Mesurier relax during a break in filming.

script to him with a note saying: "Here's one that you can read in the rehearsal room, and another to put under your pillow in the hope that something filters through during the night!" He wasn't amused,' laughs David.

One of the qualities of *Dad's Army* is its timeless humour, which makes for good clean family viewing, something which must have pleased Arthur who didn't appreciate material that was in the slightest bit suggestive or risqué. Jimmy recalls an incident in his favourite episode *The Deadly Attachment*, when

Arthur refused to have a bomb put down his trousers.

'In the original script Mainwaring had the bomb in his trousers, down which Frazer had to put his arm. Arthur never read his scripts until the last minute, and while we were on location having breakfast at the Bell Hotel, Thetford, he started rustling his script. He said: "James, could you spare a minute, please." I went over and he mumbled: "I'm not having this, I'm not having a bomb down my trousers." I reminded him that we were filming in an hour and enquired why he hadn't read the script before now? He replied that that was his concern and restated that he wasn't having a bomb down his trousers, and certainly not John Laurie's arm!'

David Croft arrived and Jimmy broke the news. They were left with little alternative but to rewrite the scene. When the episode was transmitted, it was Corporal Jones who finished up with the bomb down his trousers.

The rest of the casting was down to David Croft and Michael Mills, who was responsible for bringing John Laurie's name into the frame. Perry explains: 'Michael said: "I've got you John Laurie." To me, John Laurie was a legend. A great Shakespearean actor and one of the finest supporting actors I knew. But then came the embarrassment: his character was described simply as "A Scotsman"! Not exactly inspiring for an actor of his standing.'

Initially there were plans to make Frazer a fisherman, but Jimmy and David felt there was insufficient depth in the characterisation and chose the job of undertaker.

Arnold Ridley was selected to play the incontinent Private Godfrey because he'd worked for David Croft on *Hugh and I*. 'He was terribly funny and a lovely actor.

'I was keen on Jimmy Beck for Walker, while Ian Lavender, who was one of my wife's clients, had just played a marvellous part in *Flowers At My Feet*. He was obviously a good actor and as young as we could go for Pikey.'

When it came to Jack Jones, the butcher, David Croft agreed with Jimmy that Jack Haig, who subsequently made a handful of appearances in the series, was the ideal candidate. 'The trouble was he'd just been offered 26 programmes of *Whacky Jacky*, a character he more or less created himself for children, and that's the part he accepted,' David recalls. 'So we offered the part to Clive Dunn, who'd played a lovely old man in *Bootsie and Snudge*.' It is also reported that David Jason had unsuccessfully

Jonesey (Clive Dunn).

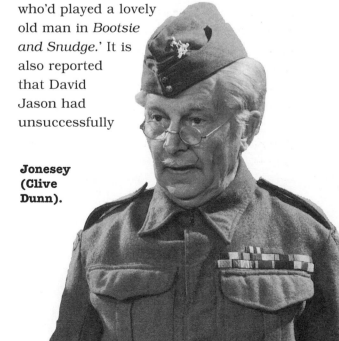

read for the part of Jones.

'Michael Mills suggested John Le Mesurier and wanted him to play the captain. But then we came up with the idea of switching the classes, and he was cast as Sergeant Wilson. John was an extraordinary performer because he never seemed totally with it. But he was a very clever man, always word-perfect and at rehearsals 15 minutes before everyone else.'

David Croft knew that Bill Pertwee possessed a tremendous sense of humour and was a great enthusiast, so was ideal for the cast. 'He's a bubbly character and one of his functions was to make the others happy, and he achieved that. He's

a lovely man and one of the few actors who never rang me up asking whether there's anything for them in the next show – he knew I'd use him when I could.

'I've cast Frank Williams in clerical roles several times before and he's a marvellous actor. I'd used Edward Sinclair as a short-sighted funeral director before, and he was terribly funny as the verger. His partnership with the vicar was wonderful.'

As far as the setting was concerned, clearly the series had to be based in a coastal town in southern England, the region closest to the Nazi threat a few miles across the English Channel. Jimmy thought up the name Brightsea-on-Sea,

but this was changed to Walmington-on-Sea before the first episode got under way. 'I pictured a small seaside town along the coast from Folkestone, an area of the world I know well,' says Jimmy. But location shooting took place not on the South Coast but in Norfolk, and there were specific reasons for this, as David Croft explains. 'We started filming in April and wanted somewhere that had lots of evergreen because it was supposed

Hodges (Bill Pertwee) with the vicar (Frank Williams).

Ian Lavender played Pike, a 'stupid boy'.

with wives usually accompanying their husbands to Norfolk. An essential part of the set each season was the chairs set aside for the principal actors, the only people allowed to use them. Kay Beck recalls being reminded by her husband of this fact.

'When I first went on location with him he took me on one side and said: "We have these special chairs and not even you are allowed to sit on them. If you'd accidentally sat on it there's no way I could've told you to move, so I thought I'd better warn you."

'He was being so gentle because he thought I wouldn't understand this!' she laughs. 'Jimmy was later given his chair, and I still have it.' Location shooting usually involved a fortnight in Norfolk, although everything could have been wrapped up in

to be summer. We also wanted to film undisturbed and the big battle areas around Thetford were ideal.

'There were rumours that East Anglia was picked because I lived there, but that's incorrect,' smiles David. 'I did buy a house there, but that was after filming had already begun.'

Filming was certainly a family affair

about ten days. Ian Lavender once asked producer David Croft why. 'He replied: "You haven't seen each other for nine months, so the nights sitting around talking after dinner are very important because you get rid of all your stories. Then when we get to the rehearsal room, we just work."'

The Jimmy Perry – David Croft partnership was ideally suited to the development of a programme such as *Dad's Army.* Perry brought an incredible

Frazer interrupts a top-level meeting.

enthusiasm and firsthand knowledge of the Home Guard to the partnership whereas Croft's professional background in TV meant he knew what sort of jokes and visual effects would work on the small screen.

Writing 30-minute episodes for a bunch of actors eager for their fair share of lines, particularly as their characters developed, threw up a constant challenge for Jimmy Perry and David Croft. Actor Ian Lavender often found weeks where there wasn't much to do, but he didn't mind.

'We all knew that eventually we'd get a bite of the cherry. For one episode I found I might only have four lines but the next focused entirely around my character – that's the way it worked. All the characters had a share of the lines

eventually. We accepted that because there's no way everyone could have hundreds of lines each episode.'

And so came the first day of location filming, a memorable day for Jimmy Perry. The *Dad's Army* team was blessed with brilliant weather throughout the years of location shooting, but the first day back in April 1968 was a cruel exception – it was snowing!

'We were trying to get the first shot in the can and waited and waited,' he says. 'David owned a Rolls Royce in those days and had parked it in a field. It was full up: Arthur, John Le Mesurier and several others were sitting in it.

'It was 11am by the time we were ready to shoot and David asked me to get everyone together. Because this was my first TV series, I was very enthusiastic and my one bugbear was that many of the cast didn't seem to share my enormous, mad, eccentric enthusiasm.

'The windows of the Rolls were steamed up as I pulled open one of the doors. Everyone was sitting there looking bellicose, and I was given the most terrible glares. I told them we were ready to film in ten minutes, and Arthur replied: "We'll come when we're ready."

'I went back to David and told him they were on the way before adding: "We've got a miserable lot of old sods here." But overall, we didn't have much trouble on the set. Some would mutter and get a bit sullen, but nothing to worry about.'

Over the years everyone got to know each other well. One of the things Jimmy Perry remembers about Arthur Lowe was his insatiable appetite. 'He loved his grub,' says Jimmy. 'He'd have a full English breakfast, wade through bacon and sausage sandwiches at the 11 o'clock break, followed by a full lunch.

'For afternoon tea it would be Mr Kipling cakes and cucumber sandwiches. And back at the hotel, he enjoyed browsing through the pile of menus to select his evening meal.

'One day we had a young floor manager working with us, and Arthur asked whether I'd told him about the Mr Kipling cakes. I hadn't, so Arthur insisted I did because he didn't want any misunderstandings, it had to be Mr Kipling's cakes. We always ended up with a wide selection of those particular cakes on location!'

Arthur was often late when it came to setting off for location shooting, and eventually it was decided that Jimmy would drive him. 'He'd often come out of the hotel doing up his belt, and breathing heavily, saying: "These early mornings play havoc with my lavatorial arrangements." I told him to eat bran for breakfast. He replied: "Oh, I wouldn't take that muck, it's like mattress stuffing."

'So I bought a packet and gave it to Arthur. About four days later he came out on time, and said: "Eating bran has changed my life!" He was a wonderful character.'

As the years passed, Jimmy Perry and David Croft were delighted with how the series developed and are happy people continue to ask about *Dad's Army*, even though they've written other TV shows. But the programme wasn't an instant hit, it took several series to establish itself.

The first series employed a newsreel style to open each episode, providing a documentary flavour to the show. When the second series was transmitted in 1969, this had been revised, Jimmy Perry explains why. 'David and I felt that we had to show the audience quickly what the series was about and using a newsreel style helped. When everyone knew the series well enough, we changed the format.'

The screening of episode one met with mixed reactions from the Press, and an audience survey arranged by David Croft revealed some negative views. 'It was a terrible reaction,' he admits. 'I think the most positive comment was: "quite like it", while most people said things like: "Don't the authors know the war's over?"'

Luckily, David had the foresight to suppress the results and prevent them reaching the higher echelons of the BBC. 'If people got to hear about it there would probably have been no second series.'

The positive, family-like atmosphere on the programme was eventually shattered by the death of Jimmy Beck, one of the public's favourite characters. Casting a shadow over the production, it was a distressing time for all. 'But we had to get the show out and ended up rewriting scenes on the spot,' says David.

Walker's absence in the episode *The Recruit*, recorded after his death, is explained via a note left on the church hall floor. Thankfully,

there was never any intention to engage another actor to replace Jimmy Beck. The part was dropped and for the seventh season a new character, Mr Cheeseman, played by Welsh actor Talfryn Thomas, was introduced. But the move wasn't successful and by the eighth series, he'd gone.

'Talfryn was a good actor but his character got too many laughs,' says David. 'We made a mistake: it was wrong

Jimmy Beck, the artist, with his wife Kay.

introducing such a strong character to a series that had been running several years. Cheeseman was an irritating character. It wasn't Talfryn's fault, it was just how Cheeseman had been created.'

Jimmy believes the character wasn't particularly popular with other cast members. 'He was too funny. No one said anything but I sensed the rest of the cast felt he had too many laughs.'

Although the show ran for nine years there were times when the cast were unsure whether a new series was to be written. The programme reached an important juncture in its life at the close of 1975 when the stage show gave Jimmy and David a welcome break from the challenges of script writing.

It gave them a chance to step back and consider the programme's future – a decision influenced by David Attenborough, who was then controller of BBC1. He persuaded them to continue. 'He took us to lunch and simply said we couldn't let the show go. He's a very persuasive man so we carried on,' David recalls.

The question always being asked is why *Dad's Army* has retained its appeal while other shows from the same genre and era have drifted into obscurity.

When you examine the success of this golden sitcom, it doesn't take long to realise its ingredients were propitious for a successful series.

Jimmy Perry believes this success is partly because he wrote about a subject he knew, and that the series reflected Britain at its best. David Croft, meanwhile, says: 'I don't think the basis of comedy changes, and it was universal family entertainment. Jimmy and I were both well-versed in pantomime and summer show comedy and an enormous amount of the show was based on that style of humour.'

In fact, whatever aspect of this perennial favourite you consider, it's clear that *Dad's Army* is perfect family viewing in every respect.

The show is predominantly a character-driven series, not a gag-driven series and, therefore, the characters with all their idiosyncrasies and foibles remain funny and won't be victims of old age.

One trademark was its ample supply of gentle humour. But occasionally Perry and Croft would write an episode that varied the mood. While a string of episodes would contain pure slapstick farce, the next might be a gentle character excursion exploring more serious themes.

A good example is the episode *Branded*, where Godfrey is sent to Coventry for admitting he was a conscientious objector during the Great War. When the episode was first transmitted, many viewers wrote congratulating Jimmy and David on their treatment of such a delicate issue.

Whenever a serious or straight scene was required, Jimmy and David could certainly deliver the goods, as Ian Lavender points out. 'The scene might only last two minutes, and may not contain a serious social slant, but when required they could write such scenes beautifully.'

Another well-crafted example is *Mum's Army*, an episode full of pathos. Making a guest appearance was Carmen Silvera, who later played Edith Artois in *'Allo, 'Allo.* 'I'd worked for David in *Hugh and I* and *Beggar My Neighbour,* so when he rang saying he'd written a special episode of *Dad's Army* and wanted me to play Mrs Gray, I was absolutely thrilled,' she says.

But when the episode, which saw Mainwaring being tempted into a brief encounter by the attractiveness of Mrs Gray, was transmitted it met with negative reactions from certain quarters of the Press, as Carmen explains: 'They didn't think it was funny enough and questioned its serious nature. But David didn't mind and still classes it as one of his favourites. What's interesting is that critics have grown to love the episode.

'Many people have written to me about it. Only last week I received a letter from an American couple asking about my time on the episode.'

During its 80-episode run, more than 200 artists appeared in the series. Often familiar faces and well-established actors would be recruited for a single episode. Actor Jonathan Cecil, who appeared in just one episode, *Things That Go Bump In The Night*, remembers that filming in front of a live audience with the main cast didn't possess its normal air of nervousness. He recalls: 'It was a wonderful atmosphere, and I've never experienced anything like it since.

'Usually one is fraught with nerves when recording in front of a live audience but that wasn't the case with *Dad's Army.* The audience loved the cast so much, they felt at ease and this rubbed off on anyone else appearing in the show.'

Just like his father before him, Jonathan continues to appreciate the humour of the series. 'I know that if I turn on *Dad's Army*, it doesn't matter at which point or whether I've seen it before, I'll always find it amusing.'

Such is the quality of every episode that many people find it difficult to select a favourite. One of the most popular and best remembered is *Deadly Attachment*, containing the memorable scenes with Philip Madoc as a U-boat captain.

Madoc enjoyed appearing in the series. 'It's startling that even though I've played many of the great classical roles during my career, it's the U-boat captain in *Dad's Army* for which I'm best remembered.'

Reflecting on the success of the series, there's only two things David Croft would have done differently. 'First, I would have employed more extras because the streets of Walmington-on-Sea were always deserted. The trouble is they're expensive: you've got to find them, dress them, feed them and pay them and it was money we didn't have.

'And second, I would have used more incidental music. That's expensive as well,' he says. 'One had to economise so on *Dad's Army* we used archival music and it worked well.' Bud Flanagan was hired to sing the famous signature tune. His fee was £105 and it was recorded in February 1968, but it took longer than expected, as David Croft explains. 'We were very lucky to get him because he was reaching the end of his career. It turned out he'd never recorded a song that he hadn't actually sung before.

'We sent him the song and he turned up as planned for the recording session with the military band. Suddenly he

realised that he didn't know the song. He was terribly apologetic about the whole thing, but in the end that signature tune was an accumulation of about eight takes pieced together.'

The series finally ended in 1977 with the episode *Never Too Old*. Although Jimmy and David knew it was time to stop, the final recording was still an emotional event. Susan Belbin, now a BBC producer of shows like *One Foot In The Grave*, was the assistant floor manager that evening. 'It was so moving I had to leave the studio because I was crying so much,' she says.

'As well as realising that this was the end of a wonderfully successful series, Jimmy and David's writing made me think about the war and the grit of the people who were the real Dad's Army. It was an emotional time.'

The platoon raise a toast.

Getting On Air

The memos shown here reveal the **BBC's** first thoughts about *Dad's Army*. The rest is televisual history.

FROM: H.C.L.E.Tel., 4144 T.C.   3700/1

SUBJECT: DAD'S ARMY: ALTERATION TO CAPTIONS   May 23rd 1968

                               Copy to: H.L.E.a.

TO: C.BBC-1

As requested by you, following C.Tel.P.'s viewing of the first of this series, the amendments listed below will be made to the opening and closing titles of this series.

1) The shots (2) of refugees in the opening titles will be replaced.

2) The shots of Nazi troops (with the captions and the artists super-imposed) will be replaced by something entirely innocuous.

Having established that your wishes are going to be carried out, I would like to record my profound disquiet over your decision. This is the first "new-look" programme on BBC-1 for which I have been responsible, and I am shocked about the alteration required(in 2 above). The whole object of this comedy series is to contrast the pathetic, comic, but valorous nature of the Home Guard, who believed at the time that this (the Nazi hordes) was what they were up against. It seems to me to be not only right but essential that this fact is brought home to the viewers - and it is, surely, our justification for doing a comedy programme on this subject.

Looking, as I do, at the abrasive nature of some of the output of other departments in the BBC television service I cannot help wondering whether we, in the Comedy Department, are controlled by different standards, i.e. clowns must stay clowns.

In any case this decision cannot help but have a depressing effect upon me and upon some other people working in this department. The thought that other departments in television are allowed to advance their output into new areas, while we, apparently, are not, can only have a bad effect in the long run.

(Michael Mills)

sw

                 Controller BBC-1

                      6067 TC

          "DAD'S ARMY" : ALTERATION TO CAPTIONS

   H.C.L.E.Tel.

                                  Copy to:

                                  27th May 196

Quite frankly, I was surprised by some points in your no of 23rd May. Although I feel it would be more profitable to continue our discussion from two armchairs, I am quite prepared say this on paper:-

1. I felt slightly uneasy about this series, as you know, whe it was first discussed. The titles underlined this view: I am sorry we differ.

2. A comparison with the output of other departments is both invidious and irrational.

3. "Different standards" for Comedy department, you allege. From the department that produced "Till Death", that's pretty rich.

4. After what I have seen so far, I think one must be allowed to wonder whether "Dad's Army" does indeed 'advance Comedy's output into new areas'. Is this really breakthrough territory?

PAUL FOX

(Paul Fox)

rms

These extracts are taken from the very first script. This was the episode the BBC considered before deciding to commission the series.

"THE FIGHTING TIGERS"
(Or Confessions Of A Home Guard Sergeant.)
By Jimmy Perry

CAST

MEMBERS OF THE 1st PLATOON BRIGHTSEA-ON-SEA HOME GUARD

SERGEANT ARTHUR WILSON (50) Chief Clerk at the Swallow Bank.
CAPTAIN GEORGE MAINWARING (50) Manager at the Swallow Bank. (Arthur Lowe.)
L/CPL. JONES (70) Owner of the local butchers shop (Robert Dorning) (Jack Haig)
PTE. FRANK PIKE (17) (Looks about 14.) Officeboy
PTE. JOE WALKER (45) Bookmaker (Arthur English) who, in order to keep the comedy moving, only speak when absolutely necessary, but must be, real characters, either very young, or over 45.
8 OTHER PRIVATES

OTHERS
MRS. PIKE (40) A smart widow, Frank Pike's mother.
GEORGE JONES Twin brother of Jim Jones (Jack Haig)
LANDLORD OF "THE CASE IS ALTERED" PUBLIC HOUSE,
1st IRISHMAN

WILSON
Yes, I remember, sir. It was a terrible disappointment.

MAINWARING
Anyhow, I've drawn up another list that I think should do the trick.
(HANDS HIM THE LIST)

WILSON
(READING) Hmmm! One revolver. Who's that for?

MAINWARING
Me of course. I'm the officer.

WILSON
Couldn't I have one too sir?

MAINWARING
Certainly not. The Tommy gun's for you.

WILSON
You mean like those American gangsters have? (HOLDING IMAGINARY TOMMY GUN) Stick 'em up you guys, this is a showdown. Rat-tat-tat-tat-tat.

MAINWARING
Wilson, pull yourself together. Remember where you are.

WILSON
Sorry sir.

MAINWARING
Now get that list off to the War Office tonight and mark it urgent.

WILSON
Very well sir. (HE GOES)

MAINWARING
(LOOKS AROUND OFFICE AND PUTS ON A SNEER) Alright you guys, this town isn't big enough for the two of us.
(DRAWS IMAGINARY REVOLVER.) Let 'em have it. Bang. Bang. Bang.
(FADE)

5. INT. H.G. H.Q. NIGHT.

(PLATOON IS GATHERED ROUND A BLACKBOARD ON WHICH IS A LARGE DRAWING OF A GERMAN TANK BRISTLING WITH GUNS. SGT. WILSON IS GIVING A LECTURE.)

SGT.
Now men, this is the German Mark II Anaconda Tank. You will observe the following points. Heavily armoured with four inch plating. One six inch repeating cannon. Two heavy machine guns and four light machine guns, one high pressure flame-thrower,

SGT. (cont.)
(FAN ROUND ON BLANK FACES.)
Well, these are our weapons men.
One blanket, one tin of petrol, beer bottles filled with petrol, and one crowbar, two petrol bombs, one box of matches. We are all under cover. follows... The procedure is as We hear the tank coming. As it draws level the tank man pours petrol over the blanket and sets light to it, breaks cover and throws the flaming blanket into the tank's tracks. This will immobilise it. Now, for this job we want a young lad of the Commando breed, that's you Pike. The next man will then break cover and prise open the lid of the tank with the crowbar. That's you Duck. Then you, L/Cpl. Jones, with another lad, will light the petrol bombs and drop them into the apperture. Now, are there any questions?
(MORE BLANK STARES.)

L/CPL. JONES
What will you be doing Sgt.?

SGT.
I shall be observing from behind cover. Right. Now let's try it. through by numbers. Pike, get down in the corner behind that packing case and take the blanket and petrol with you. (PIKE DOES SO)
Pte Fish and you three men will be the tank.(THEY EXCHANGE LOOKS) Duck, get ready with the crowbar and you Cpl. Jones grab the bombs and stand by.
(PTE. FISH AND THREE PRIVATES GO TO THE FAR END OF THE HUT. DUCK AND JONES CROUCH DOWN BESIDE PIKE.)

PIKE
Do you want me to put the petrol on the blanket now Sgt.?

SGT.
Of course not, you stupid boy. This is a dummy run.

PIKE
It's just as well 'cos the tin's empty.

SGT.
What do you mean empty? It was full yesterday. I used all our petrol ration filling the can and the two bombs.
(DURING THIS L/CPL. JONES TAKES THE STOPPERS OUT OF THE BOTTLES AND SMELLS THEM.)

2978/80
Tel.

ARTHUR LOWE

CAPTAIN MAINWARING

Captain George Mainwaring's dedication and hard work are perhaps the principal reasons he's become a pillar of society in the community of Walmington-on-Sea. Bank manager, self-appointed captain of the Home Guard, his grammar school education has rewarded him well. But his humble background and lack of experience on the fighting front often lead to bouts of insecurity, particularly when dealing with Sergeant Wilson, whom he claims was born with a silver spoon in his mouth.

Mainwaring, who's a Freemason, lives with his wife, Elizabeth, and cat, Empress. He has no children. Undoubtedly henpecked, he often gets his ear chewed off by his beloved when she calls him at the Church Hall, much to the merriment of Wilson. Any resistance to her demands is met with an abrupt drop of the receiver.

Defending her regular non-appearance at functions, Mainwaring always claims Elizabeth, who makes bizarre lampshades, is sensitive to criticism and has delicate skin.

Parading with the platoon is the highlight of his day, partly because it gives a welcome break from his missus.

Mainwaring's father Edmund, who George claimed was a member of The Master Tailors' Guild, in fact owned a little draper's shop in East Street, Eastbourne. His other son, Barry, the black sheep of the family, is a drunk who travels the country selling jokes and carnival novelties. Barry disliked George, calling him 'po-face' and claiming he was a loser as a child, always reading and taking cold baths.

Despite his shortcomings, no one can knock Captain Mainwaring's valorous attitudes. Although there's a dearth of medals on his chest, he'd be first to stand up in defence of his country. As a 2nd Lieutenant during the Great War, he arrived in France with the Pioneer Corps, 48 hours after Armistice. Age has prevented him grabbing his piece of the action this time, but he pursues his duties in the Home Guard with the utmost efficiency. Well, the intention's always there!

Captain Mainwaring and Arthur Lowe were a match made in heaven. Arthur stamped his unique style and mannerisms all over the character, making it impossible to think of anyone else playing the part; it's difficult to accept that he was only third choice to play the role, after Thorley Walters and Jon Pertwee had declined the job.

Arthur hadn't done much TV for the Beeb and Michael Mills — then BBC's Head of Comedy — wasn't convinced he was right for the part of Mainwaring. There was a belief that people who worked for the BBC did not work in commercial TV, and, of course, Arthur was from the Granada stable of actors, thanks to *Coronation Street* and *Pardon the Expression*. Fortunately the powers that be decided to give Arthur the nod.

32

Arthur Lowe in a scene with Pamela Cundell.

Born in Hayfield, Derbyshire, in 1915, Arthur – the only son of a railwayman – worked as a stagehand at the Manchester Palace of Varieties during his teenage years. He enjoyed his brush with the acting world, but never considered it a serious career option. 'He was expected to do something more managerial,' says Arthur's son, Stephen. 'But Dad was something of an adventurer and wanted to break away from the mould. A great romantic, particularly about the sea, he considered life in the Merchant Navy.'

Sadly, poor eyesight thwarted his ambitions and he worked at an aeroplane factory before joining the army on the eve of the Second World War. Whilst serving abroad in the Middle East, Arthur began taking part in shows put on for the troops. He enjoyed the experience so much that as soon as he was demobbed, he set

about making a career out of acting, at the advanced age of 30. By the time Arthur made his stage debut at a Manchester rep in 1946, he was already balding, making him well suited to character parts. 'He didn't have a striking face,' admits Stephen, 'but like all good character actors his face was like putty. He seemed able to alter it to interpret any part.'

After years of slogging away in the provinces he made his West End debut in 1950, by which time he'd already made a handful of films. His portly appearance and bumbling disposition were regularly requested and in a career covering over 30 years, he was seen in hundreds of plays and more than 50 films, including *Kind Hearts and Coronets, The Green Man, This Sporting Life* and *Man About the House.* Arthur also conquered the transition into small screen acting. Besides *Dad's Army,* two roles he'll be remembered for are draper Leonard Swindley in *Coronation Street,* and the cantankerous Redvers Potter in BBC's sitcom, *Potter.*

Working with Arthur in *Coronation Street* was William Roache, alias Ken Barlow. 'Arthur was a very private man who didn't enjoy his celebrity status,' says William. 'I grew to like him and respect his work. All his little throwaway lines were carefully worked out.

'I remember once he was sitting in the first-class compartment of a train to London after thinking he'd finished work for the week. He'd just opened a small bottle of red wine, unwrapped some bread and cheese when a police escort arrived to whisk him back to Granada studios – he still had more lines to record. Arthur was not amused!'

When offered the chance of playing Swindley, Arthur didn't relish the thought of travelling to Manchester. 'I think he would have refused the job had it not been for his agent applying pressure,' says Stephen Lowe. Fortunately for Arthur, he accepted the role.

After the success of his *Coronation Street* role, Arthur was given his own series, *Pardon the Expression,* in 1965. 'He enjoyed every role he played. The theatre was the medium with which

COLIN BEAN
(b. Wigan)
Role: Private Sponge (28 episodes); many others in non-speaking role

After leaving school in 1944 Colin joined the army for four years and began acting while serving in Japan. Graduated from drama school in 1952. Stayed on to teach for a year before joining Sheffield Rep as ASM. Worked with the Court Players for four years.

Early career dominated by theatre. First TV speaking role in 1961's *Richard the Lionheart* with Richard Greene. Played policemen in *Z Cars* and *No Hiding Place* before *Dad's Army*. Also seen in *The Liver Birds*, *Are You Being Served?*, *The Goodies*, *The Harry Worth Show* and 14 episodes of *Michael Bentine's Potty Time* in 1973. Seen in the penultimate episode of *Hi-De-Hi!* in 1988 as the verger alongside Frank Williams (as the vicar) at Gladys' wedding. Also made three films.

Working for Jimmy Perry at Watford's Palace Theatre in 1962 led to a non-speaking part in *Dad's Army*. Colin, who gained a Master's degree in Speech and Projection during the 1980s via a correspondence course, knows Sponge was never Brain of Britain, but viewed him as an ordinary, kind-hearted farmer. Arthritis now restricts Colin to radio work.

he was most at home, but filmwork was his true love,' says Stephen.

John Barron, who worked with Arthur in *Potter,* has fond memories of that time. 'Arthur was an outstanding actor who had a marvellous sense of the ridiculous combined with an unrivalled dramatic talent. I first worked with him back in 1949 at the Grand Theatre, Croydon. He always enjoyed the ability to play characters older than himself. *Potter* marked Arthur's genius. He made the character quite distinct from the immortal Captain Mainwaring although the two had many similar characteristics. That was one of his qualities.'

Although Arthur was seen in a lot of TV

Arthur Lowe's poor eyesight prevented him from joining the Merchant Navy.

JOHN RINGHAM
(b. Cheltenham)
Role: Bracewell (episode 1);
Capt. Bailey (episodes 11, 12, 18, 31).

When told Bracewell wouldn't become a regular character, John was pleased because he didn't want to be fettered by a long-running series; but he enjoyed dropping in occasionally as Captain Bailey. Primarily a classical actor, he's spent over 50 years in the profession, subsidising his theatrical career with TV and radio work.

During the war he joined a teenagers' amateur society performing 'highbrow' material which fuelled his enthusiasm for serious roles. Turned pro in 1948 and after 11 years' rep made his TV debut. During the 1960s appeared in *The Forsyte Saga*, *The Railway Children*, *War and Peace* and *David Copperfield*.

After *Dad's Army*, John worked with Arthur Lowe on several occasions, including the sitcom *Bless Me, Father*. Recently seen in an episode of *The Governor* and an advert for vegetarian sausages. Has made over 200 theatre appearances, including the National, 300 TV roles and one film, 1961s *Very Important Person*.

John is still working on TV and in the theatre; he also writes plays.

parts, for most people he'll always be remembered as Mainwaring, leader of the Walmington-on-Sea Home Guard. Thanks to his delightful idiosyncrasies he injected an incredible vividness into the role: with a perfectly timed pause, glance, puff, or rub of his red rotund face, he could have the audience and viewers in stitches.

When *Dad's Army* finished, Arthur – who refused to allow a script in his home – shared in the sadness marking the end of the series, as Stephen explains. 'By then, Jimmy Beck had died, John Le Mesurier was unwell and no one had expected the series to last as long as it did anyway. But he was sad at the passing of an era.'

In his later years, Arthur was in a position to pick and choose his work. Although he made a great success of his

Captain Mainwaring discusses tactics.

career, Stephen Lowe believes he could have achieved much more but for his tendency to decline work if a part in the production couldn't be found for his wife, Joan, who also appeared in *Dad's Army*. 'Her performance was not in the same class as Arthur's, and the stance he took limited what he did.'

Away from the spotlight, Arthur was not dissimilar to Mainwaring in many ways. 'He could be pompous at times,' says Stephen. 'and was always dapperly dressed as well. He carried a briefcase to work, which was incredibly tidy, and a pair of nail clippers in his pocket.'

Arthur died in 1982 after suffering a stroke in the dressing room of Birmingham's Alexandra Theatre, where he was performing *Home at Seven*. That day the world lost one of its greatest character actors.

PERRY ON LOWE
Arthur and I had one thing in common: we'd both done years in weekly rep; it's something unheard of today: a permanent company doing a fresh play every week the whole year round. For actors, it was a make or break experience. If you survived it gave you tremendous ability to time your performance and Arthur's comic timing was amongst the greatest I've ever seen.

Setting the Scene

For any TV show production staff are crucial to its success: a skilled, well-organised team provide the essential support, resources and expertise needed to bring a programme to life. Two departments playing a major part in the *Dad's Army* legend were the design and visual effects teams.

Paul Joel was one of the linchpins in the design team, working on six series and one Christmas Special. 'My role involved designing sets, such as The Marigold Tea Rooms or Jones' shop, and dressing the locations being used in Norfolk. I was also involved in actually selecting some of the locations.'

When designing a set, Paul not only researched fastidiously, but drew on his own experience and memories. 'For Jones' butcher's shop, I remembered seeing shops years ago that were tiled in the most elaborate way. The tiles were so colourful it seemed as if they'd got an artist to paint them,' he says.

'For the TV series I chose to decorate them in a Victorian style: the tiles were highly decorative, amusing and evocative of the butcher's trade. I made up a design and an artist painted it on the tiles. I was pleased with the results and it helped make a highly decorative interior which suited Jones' florid personality.'

When it came to designing Walmington's branch of Swallow Bank the displacement of space was predetermined in many ways by the script, but Paul was still influenced by his childhood memories of the first postwar banks.

The greatest challenge he faced occurred in the episode *Time On My Hands*, which involved an enemy pilot hanging from the town clock. The set, which was built in the studio, was extremely complex and costly in comparison with others in the series.

'That episode would probably have eaten up most of the money allocated for that series. If there was a particularly expensive episode like that one, Jimmy and David usually made sure the rest in the series were cheap to set up.

'There was a lot of elaborate machinery involved in *Time On My Hands*, the sort of thing attempted in a movie with plenty of money and time, but we had to complete it overnight. It was certainly the most difficult set I worked on.'

Paul, who now works as a freelance designer, loved working on the programme. As the series progressed, he felt Jimmy Perry and David Croft presented him with more and more challenges. 'They got more difficult as time went on, but challenges like that bring out the best in people.'

Early on in the show, Paul was responsible for finding Jones' butcher's van. It was just about driveable but needed renovation, a task Paul undertook. 'It was of the right vintage and crying out to have some elaborate graphics on it which would correspond with his shop. I found it in the Surrey area and was pleased with the result.'

Whenever an episode needed special effects, a designer such as Peter Day, who worked on over four series, was called for. Very much a hands-on designer, he'd get amongst the thick of the action.

Battle School, a part of which was subsequently used in the programme's closing credits, shows Mainwaring and his platoon weaving across open ground while explosions erupt all around. Just out of camera pressing buttons to fire the smoke, which was usually gun powder or fireworks, was Peter.

'I always tried making the explosions as realistic as possible. In one episode, a firework was placed underneath small bags of cement. When it blew up, spouts of grey smoke filled the air – it made a very good effect.'

From a safety angle, Peter planned his work meticulously. 'On one episode we had explosions placed up the side of a hill. This was fine, but one or two of the extras in the platoon were keen to get themselves seen on camera, and would occasionally stray from the rest.

'I remember warning one of them not to

This set is just one example of the design team's hard work.

go too far up the hill because that was where we'd set the explosions. After going too close he ended up covered in brown powder. He certainly got himself noticed, though not on camera. *Dad's Army* was a great series to work on.'

JOHN LE MESURIER

Arthur Wilson is chief clerk at Walmington-on-Sea's branch of Swallow Bank, and sergeant of the town's Home Guard unit. In charge of both is pompous Mr Mainwaring, who always seems to suffer Wilson's sublime skills in unintentional one-upmanship.

Wilson's languid, self-effacing style bugs his superior immensely. While Mainwaring treats life seriously, Wilson views it with an air of equanimity verging on the blasé, and that irks.

With a public school education, he began his banking career before serving in the army during the Great War. After demob, he returned to banking. While working in Weston-super-Mare, he met Mrs Pike, who followed him to Walmington upon his promotion to chief clerk. A stray bomb put paid to Wilson's short-lived role as bank manager at the Eastgate branch. Now it seems inevitable that his career is destined to linger under the heavy thumb of Mainwaring.

Wilson's relationship with Mrs Pike and her son, Frank, is always the cause of gossip around the town. Even if he isn't Frank's father, his avuncular approach is warmly welcomed by mum and son alike.

Whenever John Le Mesurier was offered a job, it always felt like returning to school. His widow, Joan, explains: 'Enthusiasm was never one of his qualities. He suffered quiet despair whenever asked to play something. Often he'd say: "I just wish the studio would burn down, without hurting anyone, of course." He suffered this trepidation every time.'

So when the offer to assume the role of Sergeant Wilson came along, John didn't exactly jump at the chance. 'There was no romance in the series, and hardly any women, so John thought it wouldn't last,' says Joan. 'He kept phoning Clive Dunn and discussing it, but there wasn't really any chance of him turning it down. And I'm glad he didn't because he loved the programme.'

John admired the ensemble recruited for the series, and enjoyed meeting up with everyone each season, particularly for location shooting. 'He likened it to going on holiday with the Boys' Club,' says Joan. 'I went along quite often and the atmosphere was wonderful.'

Initially, the question of how to play Wilson foxed John. Eventually, he decided the only way was to base the character on his own experience in the army. With the occasional jacket button undone, cuff turned up, commands issued like invitations, the affable Arthur Wilson was born. 'Everything John did was a variation on a theme of himself, he couldn't do it any other way; that's how he tackled any role.'

Even though John turned his back on a law career – both his father and grandfather had been lawyers – in preference for acting, he never regretted the decision once. Joan says: 'He loved acting, and was very happy. Anyway, I don't think he was cut out to be a lawyer.'

Born in Bedford in 1912, John attended

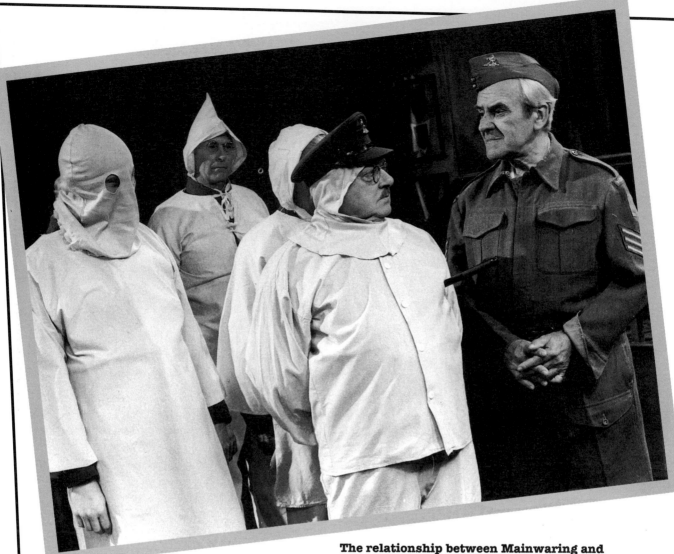

The relationship between Mainwaring and Wilson was frequently prickly.

Sherborne School, Dorset, before embarking initially on a life in law. But he had always nurtured a secret desire to try his hand at acting, and when he was 20, his parents finally gave their blessing.

A career spanning five decades began at the Fay Compton Studio of Dramatic Art. Interrupted only by a spell in the army – he finished his service as a captain on the northwest Indian frontier – John was busy throughout his career.

His work incorporated all mediums of the acting profession, including many years of rep. But it was film work he enjoyed most. 'He loved making films,' says Joan Le Mesurier. 'Stage work frightened him as he got older, and, of course, the money was poor. He always said he couldn't afford to tour for very long because the hotels were so expensive. He liked a good hotel, but the wages didn't match the cost.'

One of John's trademarks was his tendency to appear vague and helpless, something actor

Frank Williams can vouch for. 'He was vague all over the place, and made a thing out of appearing helpless at times. I'm sure it was a ploy to get people to do things for him,' he says.

'Whilst touring with the stage show he asked what I did with dirty washing. I said I took it to a laundry. He then asked Teddy Sinclair, who took his to a launderette. When I asked what he did, he replied: "I just leave it about the room and some kind person always does it for me." That was absolutely typical of the man, deliberately helpless.'

John was a popular man, and someone fellow platoon member Ian Lavender grew to respect and admire, although at first he found him difficult to film with. 'You were dicing with death doing a scene with him,' he smiles. 'Occasionally he'd say his lines differently from how he rehearsed them – in the beginning, I didn't look forward to scenes with him.'

Away from work, Joan acknowledges that John – a keen reader and listener of jazz – liked a good joke. She recalls an incident at Thetford. 'After filming one day, everyone retired to the bar. A friend, Dinny Powell, a stuntman employed on the series, had taught John how to fall over from a standing position. He decided to try it while the bar was packed with actors and production crew.'

Although it was the cause of much consternation, John found it very amusing, partly because of the reactions he observed while lying on the floor. 'The make-up girls had his head in their laps, while the scriptwriters were terrified they'd have to write him out of the following day's scenes – he found it hilarious,' says Joan.

At the end of the final series, John was saddened by the prospect of no more *Dad's Army*. He was also miffed that the BBC didn't give the series a merited send-off, although the honour was picked up by the *Daily Mirror* who hosted a celebratory function. 'It was a wonderful night,' recalls Joan, 'the perfect end to a perfect series as far as John was concerned.'

Among his numerous TV credits, John won a BAFTA for Best Actor in the Dennis Potter play *Traitor* in 1971, even though it took Joan three weeks to persuade him to accept the part. Other appearances included: Colonel Maynard in *George and the Dragon*; Lord Bleasham in *A Class By Himself*; guest roles in *Hancock's Half Hour*; *Brideshead Revisited*; *The Goodies* and *Worzel Gummidge*. It was also his voice behind various Homepride flour commercials and Bod, the children's character.

ERIC LONGWORTH (b. Shaw)
Role: Mr Gordon (episode 53); Town Clerk (episodes 58, 62, 64, 65, 68, 74, 77)

When his father died Eric was only 17, and his ambition to become an actor were sidetracked while he helped support the family. He worked as a printer's salesman until his call-up. In 1943–44, while serving with the army in Bombay, he got involved with the dramatic society and pursued an acting career after demob.

His first professional job was at Oldham Rep, where he stayed 11 years. Eric moved behind the scenes and became Oldham theatre manager between 1951 and 1957, and Guildford's until 1963. Returning to acting, Christmas Day 1963 saw him in Granada's 90-minute epic *Mr Pickwick*, with Arthur Lowe playing the lead. This was his second TV appearance, the first being in *Shadow Squad* in the late 1950s. Eric believes his appearance in a 1972 episode of TV's *Lollipop*, written by Jimmy Perry, led to the offer of work in *Dad's Army* later that year.

Eric understudied Arthur Lowe in the *Dad's Army* stage show but didn't tour with the production. Has had a handful of minor film roles: a scene with Ursula Andress in 1970's *Perfect Friday*, *No Sex Please, We're British* and *Tom Jones*. Other TV parts include two appearances in *Coronation Street*, one playing a policeman alongside Jimmy Beck.

No recent long-running TV roles or theatre parts, but Eric, who recently celebrated 51 years in showbiz, is kept busy with commercials.

John Le Mesurier in a scene from the episode, *Knights of Madness*.

Equally adept playing serious roles as well as comedy, he scored more than 150 film credits during his long career, with classics such as *Private's Progress, I'm All Right, Jack, The Bulldog Breed* and *The Battle of the River Plate*. In fact, John became one of those familiar character faces popping up in seemingly every postwar British movie made.

John died in 1983, aged 71, he had been ill some time. While rehearsing a play – *The Miser* – in Perth, Australia, he began finding it difficult to learn lines; he blamed the intense heat until he collapsed and was rushed to hospital suffering from liver failure.

Joan, unaware of the situation, was planning to meet up with John. 'I was literally waiting for a taxi to arrive to take me to the airport when the phone rang,' she recalls. 'John's agent explained that he'd collapsed and was coming home.'

The liver failure was blamed on the cumulative affect of alcohol. 'It was very sad because although I knew John liked a drink, he was not a drunk. He liked the conviviality of jazz clubs and bars. Sadly, drinking over a number of years caused the problem.'

For a year, John followed a rigid alcohol-free diet consisting largely of fruit and salads; as a result the fat just fell of him. 'He looked ghastly,' admits Joan, 'especially during the last series of *Dad's Army*.'

Although he kept to the diet, he felt increasingly miserable. Finally, he decided enough was enough and returned to the occasional drink. Almost immediately he looked like the old John Le Mesurier, and enjoyed another five years of life before a series of liver haemorrhages saw

FREDDIE EARLLE (b. Glasgow)
Role: Henry (episode 56);
Italian Sgt. (episode 68)

Was only five when he made his first radio broadcast with his school's percussion band. Always wanted to act and worked in various amateur companies before joining the army at the start of the Second World War. Between 1943 and 1945 he toured India in a concert party, good experience for his later appearances in *It Ain't Half Hot, Mum*. After demob, set up a double-act with a friend and then his first wife. His career gradually progressed and has included variety, theatre and TV.

After his agent had persuaded him to have a nose-job to reduce its size, he made his first TV appearance wearing a false one while impersonating Jimmy Durante, renowned for his large nose!

Other TV includes: *Cool for Cats, People and Places*, children's show *Play Time*, numerous appearances in *The Bill* and various commercials. Also worked on one series of *Room Service*, written by Jimmy Perry in the late 1970s, and two of *Michael Bentine's Square World*, with Clive Dunn.

him bedridden in hospital.

'I'll never forget that on the day he died the TV in his ward was showing one of his old films. There was John lying in bed looking awful, while on screen suntanned and well in *Where The Spies Are*. The last words he said to me were: "I've had enough now, I want to die." Typical of John's humour, he ensured that his obituary announced that he had 'conked out'.

PERRY ON LE MESURIER
John's laid-back style and apparent lack of enthusiasm at times nearly drove me mad. It was only later that I realised he was a very shy man, strangely lacking in confidence. John was a consummate professional, always knew his lines and was never late. Sadly it's only now looking back over the years I realise what a wonderful contribution he made to *Dad's Army*.

Series Guide:
SEASONS 1-3

SEASON ONE

Transmitted in b/w, 31/7/68 – 11/9/68

1. THE MAN AND THE HOUR

Also appearing: Janet Davies (Mrs Pike), Caroline Dowdeswell (Janet King), John Ringham (Bracewell), Bill Pertwee (ARP Warden) Neville Hughes (Soldier).

As Anthony Eden announces the forming of the Local Defence Volunteers (LDV), Mainwaring appoints himself commander of the Invasion Committee, with Wilson second-in-command. Volunteers are enrolled at the church hall. Frazer is first, and here we encounter Wilson and Mainwaring's conflicting styles of command.

MAINWARING: Get the first man in.
WILSON: Oh, very well. *(Looking out of the office door)* Would you mind stepping this way, please.
MAINWARING: Wilson, Wilson, come here, come here. I intend to mould those men out there into an aggressive fighting unit; I'm going to lead them, command them and inspire them to be ruthless killers, and I'm not going to get very far if you invite them to step this way, am I? Quick march is the order.

The platoon fall in at the church hall.

WHAT THE PAPERS SAID!

The screening of the first ever episode of *Dad's Army* met with a lukewarm reception from the Press, who seemed undecided in their views.

'The trouble with this is that it isn't situation comedy or character comedy, it's only gag comedy, the easiest to write and the quickest wearing on the car.' **DAILY MAIL**

'As the Walmington volunteers assembled, Messrs Perry and Croft showed a real gift for satire. Two things defeated them. One was the inexcusable use of a modern studio audience: every time it reacted 1940 was lost and we were back in 1968. The other was a tendency to go for laughs at all cost, even if they punctured the atmosphere.' **THE DAILY TELEGRAPH**

'He is puffed up with importance. Bloated with mission. The hour has come. He is the man for the hour. Arthur Lowe is its kingpin. And what holds it together.' **DAILY MIRROR**

'It seemed to me to blend sentiment and humour rather uneasily as if afraid of making too much fun of a hallowed wartime institution. Whether this rather equivocal attitude to the Home Guard will pay dividends remains to be seen.' **THE TIMES**

'I cannot say I cracked a rib, split my sides or even raised a good hearty belly-laugh – but some instinct is still telling me that the BBC is about to come up with a classic comedy series.' **DAILY EXPRESS**

'It is played in such an easy-going natural fashion that one imagines even the most hard-bitten professional anti-patriots must find it amusing.' **THE GUARDIAN**

'*Dad's Army* is a nice little thing.' **THE SUN**

'I'm fairly hopeful that this may prove an interesting series, though in the opening instalment the balance between humour and nostalgia seemed to be held uneasily.' **SUNDAY TIMES**

'Jimmy Perry's and David Croft's inaugural script was pretty feeble, with an over-reliance on strained little jokes, but again this may only be a scene-setting problem.' **SUNDAY TELEGRAPH**

'My character was a smartly dressed city gent who was thick as two short planks. It was meant to be a regular part, but on the first day of rehearsals David Croft said: "We've got too many regular characters and one has got to go." And that was me. But David is a loyal man and brought me back four times as Captain Bailey.'

JOHN RINGHAM

WILSON: I'm very sorry, sir. Quick march
(By this time, Frazer has already entered the office)
FRAZER: There's no point, I'm already here.

Enrolment is wrapped up after Hodges makes his debut telling Mainwaring to clear the hall, he's got a lecture in five minutes. The first day of Walmington's LDV ends with an inspection and lecture on German tanks. The expected delivery of uniforms only brings LDV armbands.

2. MUSEUM PIECE

Also appearing: Janet Davies (Mrs Pike), Caroline Dowdeswell (Janet King), Leon Cortez (the Milkman), Eric Woodburn (Museum Caretaker) and Michael Osborne (the Boy Scout).

Six weeks to go before uniforms arrive

and the platoon's arsenal comprises of a shotgun, 15 carving knives, Jones' assegai and Bracewell's number three iron. But when a letter arrives instructing the bank to close the Peabody Museum of Historic Army Weapons' account for the duration, Mainwaring and Wilson have an idea.

At 1800 hours Operation Gun Grab begins. The aim: to requisition any firearms of use in the platoon's fight against the Nazis. The trouble is they've got to outwit the crusty 88-year-old caretaker who turns out to be Jones' father. After numerous attempts Frazer, disguised as an ARP warden, exploits the caretaker's predilection for booze. While he's outside the museum swigging down whisky, the platoon seizes a Chinese Rocket Gun. Mainwaring, who's not particularly enthused by their new weapon, is forced to eat his words when the gun goes off and he ends up sheltering under the table!

'I was about 22 when I did *Dad's Army* and extremely naïve. I gravitated towards dear old Arnold Ridley as I already knew him via my agent, but was somewhat taken aback as the old boy used to tell the most risqué of jokes. I was rather shocked, it was as if the Pope swore!'

CAROLINE DOWDESWELL

Pike and Mainwaring illustrate the value of teamwork.

3. COMMAND DECISION

Also appearing: Caroline Dowdeswell (Janet King), Geoffrey Lumsden (Colonel Square), Charles Hill (the Butler), Gordon Peters (the Soldier)

When the platoon fall in, Mainwaring tells Pike off for wearing a muffler on parade. But he's got a note from his mother.

MAINWARING: (Reading note) 'Frank is starting with his chest again, he ought to be in bed. If he can't wear his muffler he's to come home or he will catch his death.' (Turning to Wilson) We can't have him wearing that thing on parade, makes the whole platoon look ludicrous.
WILSON: Perhaps he could wear it on patrol, sir? (Turning to Pike) What time do you go on?
PIKE: Ten till twelve, sir.
WILSON: It'll be dark by then, sir, anyway.
MAINWARING: Oh, very well.

The dearth of weapons causes low morale in the platoon. At the bank the following day a visit from an old campaigner,

FRED McNAUGHTON (b. London)
Role: Mayor (episodes 56, 58, 65, 77)

A direct relative of music-hall star Marie Lloyd, Fred was the fourth generation of a theatrical family. He was training as a lawyer when his father died in 1920. Having to support his family, he began a 60-year career by joining Archie Pitt's Lido Follies as juvenile lead.

Straight man and scriptwriter for top variety double acts with first Raymond Bennett, then Stan Stanford, Fred was a radio star in the 1930s and 1940s. From 1946, he was lead comedian in provincial pantos and tours of Whitehall farces.

In the mid-1950s series like *Emergency — Ward 10*, *Dixon of Dock Green*, *Z Cars*, *Softly, Softly*, *The Plane Makers* and *Crossroads* brought him to TV, and later to films.

He was Stage Director at the London Palladium and understudied Frankie Howerd and Max Bygraves there for more than ten years. Over six feet tall, Fred was often cast in uniform on stage. Appearances include *Journey's End*, *Seagulls Over Sorrento*, *Worm's Eye View*, and in films, *Charge of the Light Brigade*.

His wide range of dialects gave him contracts at the Gate Theatre, Dublin, and countless voice-overs. A back injury, sustained when wearing full armour, slowed him down after 1978. He died in 1981 after a short illness.

ATTENTION!

'I remember John Le Mesurier often adopted the role of Grand Seigneur. I could never find a make-up girl to powder me down as they were all fussing over John. He always seemed to have about three of them around him: one doing his hair, one giving him a manicure and another running errands or getting him a sandwich. He was always so languid and would call everyone 'dear lady' in a world-wearied drawl while they fell over themselves fetching and carrying for him. As Arthur Lowe didn't appear to feature highly on their list of priorities, I later developed the idea that the make-up department was subconsciously reacting to the social class of the characters we played.'
CAROLINE DOWDESWELL

ATTENTION!

'Hugh Hastings, Colin Bean and Richard Jacques got paid an extra fiver for their horse-riding abilities in this episode. 'I'd ridden a horse since I was a boy working as a cowhand out in Australia, but the one I was given in this episode was certainly a fiery steed. During rehearsals I remember David Croft telling me I was riding too well! He wanted the platoon members to look as if they couldn't ride, so I spent the rest of the time attempting to look clumsy in the saddle – it was difficult.' **HUGH HASTINGS**

Colonel Square, leaves Mainwaring in a predicament. Square wants to take over the platoon and in doing so will allow them use of his 20 rifles. That evening, after much cogitating, Mainwaring announces he's placing the platoon under Square's command. But at Marsham Hall, Square's home, Mainwaring swiftly reverses his decision after discovering the crackpot plans to turn them into cavalry with circus horses and antiquarian muskets.

Back under Mainwaring's command their supply of guns arrive before the day's out.

Arthur Lowe in familiar pose.

4. ENEMY WITHIN THE GATES

Also appearing: Caroline Dowdeswell (Janet King), Carl Jaffe (Capt. Winogrodzki), Denys Peek and Nigel Rideout (the German pilots), Bill Pertwee (the ARP Warden), David Davenport (the Military Police Sgt.).

Mainwaring's lecture on dealing with enemy agents is interrupted by a monocle-wearing officer, with a suspicious accent. Not taking any chances, they arrest the man and plan an interrogation until he convinces them he's a Polish captain serving with GHQ - he's there simply to inform them of the £10 reward for every Nazi arrested.

On night patrol, Jones' section captures two German pilots. While being held at the church hall, Godfrey credulously lets them escape. But the Polish captain recaptures them and escorts the pilots back to the hall. When military police collect the prisoners, the Polish captain is mistakenly arrested as well, rewarding the platoon by a total of £30.

5. THE SHOWING UP OF CORPORAL JONES

Also appearing: Janet Davies (Mrs Pike), Martin Wyldeck (Major Regan), Patrick Waddington (the Brigadier), Edward Sinclair (the Caretaker), Therese McMurray (the girl at the window).

Major Regan visits from area HQ to monitor progress in everything from use of weapons to first aid. Things run smoothly until he labels Jones a potential danger: not only did he forget how to aim a rifle, but his glasses steamed up when charging the dummy with his bayonet.

Jones' fate is decided on his ability to negotiate an assault course in 15 minutes. On the eve of the test, Jones' outlook is bleak until certain platoon members cook up a plan. Strategically placed along the course, they help the butcher romp home with two minutes to spare.

ATTENTION!

'Our uniforms arrived in episode five. Everyone had been looking forward to receiving them, and when initially we were only issued armbands we were disappointed. It seemed ages before the full uniforms arrived, but they soon became the bane of our lives – they were so uncomfortable.'
IAN LAVENDER

6. SHOOTING PAINS

Also appearing: Guest Star, Barbara Windsor (Laura La Plaz) with Janet Davies (Mrs Pike), Caroline Dowdeswell (Janet King), Martin Wyldeck (Major Regan), Jimmy Perry (Charlie Cheeseman), Therese McMurray (the girl at the window).

Mainwaring and Wilson discuss the forthcoming shooting practice and the fiasco last time.

MAINWARING: To tell you the truth, Wilson, I was a bit ashamed of our shooting last week.
WILSON: *(Glancing away and rubbing his ear lobe)* Oh, I don't know, sir, some of the men didn't do too badly.

Frazer clinches victory in *Shooting Pains*.

ATTENTION!

'I remember being taken to this army firing range, and being a little scared when Harold Snoad told everyone to be careful where they walked as there could be live shells around. I kept thinking to myself: "What are the BBC thinking of!"'
THERESE McMURRAY

MAINWARING: No, I still fail to understand how they can possibly mistake the tyres on the area commander's staff car for the target.
WILSON: All four of them?
MAINWARING: No, all five of them – they got the spare as well!

Mainwaring's platoon, first to be formed in the area, is selected to provide the guard of honour for the Prime Minister's impending visit. But sloppy shooting at the range forces the major to consider changing his views and select the Eastgate platoon instead. The matter is decided by a shooting contest in which three of Walmington's men compete against Eastgate. A visit to the local Hippodrome that evening sparks off one of Walker's devious plans.

Crack shot Laura La Plaz, who entertains the Hippodrome audience with her firing skills, dresses up as a platoon member to help Walmington win the shooting contest. But when it appears the scheme is going to backfire, Frazer steps up and clinches victory by scoring five bull's-eyes.

SEASON TWO

Transmitted in b/w, 1/3/69 – 5/4/69

Sadly, all but one of the episodes (number ten) in this season have been wiped and haven't been shown since 1969. David Croft has attempted to find copies around the world but to date has had little joy.

7. OPERATION KILT

Also appearing: Janet Davies (Mrs Pike), James Copeland (Capt. Ogilvy).

While the platoon are completing their first PT lesson, Captain Ogilvy, of the Highland Regiment, arrives to brief the men on Saturday night's manoeuvres. Six of his regiment will attempt to capture Mainwaring's HQ. As the Walmington boys outnumber Ogilvy's bunch by three to one, they shouldn't have any problems; and that proves to be the case because

after spying on Ogilvy at his base at Manor Farm, the Walmington platoon are successful in laying man traps to capture their opponents.

8. THE BATTLE OF GODFREY'S COTTAGE

Also appearing: Janet Davies (Mrs Pike), Amy Dalby (Dolly), Nan Braunton (Cissy), Bill Pertwee (the ARP Warden) and Colin Bean (Private Sponge).

Godfrey's cottage is picked as a machine-gun post in the event of an invasion. While Mainwaring is in the bank's vault, he doesn't hear the toll of the church bells signifying a German invasion, or so everybody thinks. Wilson and Pike head for the Novelty Rock Emporium while Jones and Frazer inform Mainwaring and head for Godfrey's cottage, unaware of where their sergeant has gone. Eventually Wilson and Pike decide to make for the cottage, which is being guarded by the rest of the platoon. When Jones nips off to the outside toilet, Wilson and Pike mistake him for a German and begin shooting. But when Godfrey's sister, oblivious to all the pandemonium, waves her tea cloth out of the window, Wilson and Pike take it as a sign of surrender and move towards the home, only to find their supposed enemies are none other than their own men.

9. THE LONELINESS OF THE LONG-DISTANCE WALKER

Also appearing: Anthony Sharp (the Brigadier – War Office), Diana King (the Chairwoman), Patrick Waddington (the Brigadier), Edward Evans (Mr Reed), Michael Knowles (Capt. Cutts), Gilda Perry (Blonde), Larry Martyn (Soldier) and Robert Lankesheer (Medical Officer).

ATTENTION!

'When Jimmy Beck first arrived for filming episode one he was wearing a sort of tracksuit. A typing error meant the description for his costume read 'sprint suit' not 'spiv suit'. I scoured Thetford and fortunately found a shop with a 30-year-old suit. The shopkeeper was pleased because he didn't think he'd ever get rid of it!'
HAROLD SNOAD

Walker was called up in episode 9.

ATTENTION!

'Dad's Army was my introduction to TV. It was quite awe-inspiring working with actors like John Laurie and John Le Mesurier, people I'd only seen in films before, and here I was actually working with them. I was very nervous but enjoyed my time very much.'
MICHAEL KNOWLES

Walker is called up which is bad news for the platoon because of his deftness in acquiring essential supplies like cigarettes, booze and fudge for Godfrey's sister. Mainwaring decides Walker is too important to the platoon to let him go, so fights the War Office on his behalf. His valiant attempts fail and Walker joins the army. But within days he's discharged, much to the relief of the platoon, when it's discovered he's allergic to corned beef.

10. SGT. WILSON'S LITTLE SECRET

Also appearing: Janet Davies (Mrs Pike), Graham Harboard (Little Arthur).

Overhearing Mrs Pike talking to Frank, Wilson gets the wrong end of the stick. After receiving a letter from the WVS asking her to take in an evacuee, she tells Pike it will be nice being a mother again. Wilson hears and assumes Mavis is pregnant!

Confusion reigns and when Wilson eventually confides in Mainwaring, his superior sees no alternative but for Wilson to wed. The platoon's to provide the guard of honour at the wedding, but as Wilson practices the ceremonial march with Jones substituting for Mrs Pike, Mavis brings little

Arthur into the church hall and introduces him to Wilson. Confusion cleared, Wilson breathes a sigh of relief.

11. A STRIPE FOR FRAZER

Also appearing: Geoffrey Lumsden (Corporal-Colonel Square), John Ringham (Capt. Bailey), Gordon Peters (Policeman) and Edward Sinclair (the Caretaker).

Mainwaring is allowed to promote someone to corporal. He suggests that instead of giving the job to Jones, they should install another lance-corporal and see who performs the best. Classing himself as a shrewd judge of character,

Jones and Frazer were in competition in Episode 11.

Square), John Ringham (Capt. Bailey), Ernst Ulman (Sigmund Murphy),Bill Pertwee (the ARP Warden), Queenie Watts (Mrs Keane), June Petersen (Mrs Keen) and Gladys Dawson (Mrs Witt).

The platoon are on watch for fire bombs when Frazer spots a light flashing on the corner of Mortimer Street. They suspect a spy signalling to the enemy planes overhead.

Mainwaring and his men arrest the suspect, a Mr Murphy, who claims he's a British citizen even though he was born in Austria. Back at the church hall, an incendiary device lands and cause a fire that the platoon struggles to control.

It's Mrs Pike who extinguishes the fire by smothering it with sandbags. At the same time she vouches for Mr Murphy: he was married to her Auntie Ethel's cousin.

he picks Frazer, against Wilson's advice. The competition causes intense rivalry between the two candidates and much fawning towards Mainwaring. The men begin to dislike Frazer's brash attitudes and overpowering desire to impress, particularly when he presents charge sheets containing Pike's name for deserting his post and cowardice in the face of the enemy, and Walker for mutiny. After Jones is added to the list, action is required: Frazer quickly falls out of contention for promotion.

12. UNDER FIRE

Also appearing: Janet Davies (Mrs Pike), Geoffrey Lumsden (Corporal-Colonel

SEASON THREE
Transmitted 11/9/69 – 11/12/69

13. THE ARMOURED MIGHT OF LANCE CORPORAL JONES

Also appearing: Janet Davies (Mrs Pike), Bill Pertwee (the ARP Warden), Frank Williams (the Vicar), Queenie Watts (Mrs Peters), Pamela Cundell (Mrs Fox), Jean St Clair (Miss Meadows), Olive Mercer (Mrs Casson), Nigel Hawthorne (the angry man), Harold Bennett (the old man) and Dick Haydon (Raymond).

GHQ orders the platoon to work closer with the ARP. The new chief warden is to discuss suggestions as to how this can be achieved; but who is the new warden, asks Mainwaring.

WILSON: It's that rather common fellow, sir, Mr Hodges, I think.
MAINWARING: You mean to say they've made him chief warden?
WILSON: Yes, they have.
MAINWARING: He's a greengrocer!
WILSON: Yes, I know that, sir, because of his dirty fingernails.

As soon as Hodges arrives, the foundations of his friction-based relationship with Mainwaring are laid. Walker persuades Jones into loaning his delivery van, which is converted to gas for fuel economy, to the platoon, primarily because he wants to use it for his own black market dealings. The delivery van takes on a new role as an ambulance during Hodges' air raid practice, with the platoon becoming stretcherbearers.

ERIK CHITTY (b. Dover)
Role: Mr Sedgewick (episode 29); Mr Clerk (63)

Erik enjoyed his time on *Dad's Army*, partly for the chance to meet up with John Le Mesurier and Clive Dunn (he'd worked with both at The Players Theatre).

After leaving Dover College he studied Law at Cambridge in the 1920s (where he co-founded and became the first treasurer of the university's acting society), before going on to RADA.

Upon graduating he followed his dream and trod the boards for years in reps around the country, interrupted only by the war, during which he served as a sergeant in Egypt and Italy with the Eighth Army.'

Often cast as testy old men, Erik was seen on TV from as early as 1938, in *The White Chateau*. Made over 200 small screen appearances, including 1946 production of *Alice* and an eerie adaption of *Markheim*. Best known as Mr Smith, the English teacher, in *Please, Sir!*

Before he died in 1977, Erik had notched up over 40 film credits, including *Chance of a Lifetime*, *Raising a Riot*, *Casino Royale*, *The Railway Children* and *A Bridge Too Far*.

'That rather common fellow' – Warden Hodges.

ATTENTION!

'I'm sure I was offered the part of Mrs Fox because of my wink! I was playing a fortuneteller in a BBC programme and at the end of a scene winked at the camera. David Croft was in the audience, spotted the wink and liked it. So when I appeared in *Dad's Army*, one of the first things I had to do was wink at Jonesey. Mrs Fox was a woman in a queue to start with but she developed as the series progressed – she was a wonderful character.' **PAMELA CUNDELL**

14. BATTLE SCHOOL

Also appearing: Alan Tilvern (Capt. Rodrigues), Alan Haines (Major Smith), Colin Bean (Pte. Sponge).

The platoon is a train ride away from weekend camp and a course in guerrilla warfare. Mainwaring is hungry and grouchy and Godfrey uncomfortable.

GODFREY: I hope we get there soon.
MAINWARING: Why?
GODFREY: It's all very awkward this not being a corridor train . . . it's very difficult indeed.
MAINWARING: You'll just have to control yourself, Godfrey. There's a war on you know – active service.

After taking four hours to reach the camp from the station, just a mile away, the platoon's hunger pains deepen when they discover they've missed supper. After oversleeping and missing breakfast too, they set out to capture Capt. Rodrigues' base. Upon discovering a secret tunnel leading straight into the HQ, Mainwaring tells the platoon they'll capture the base at nightfall.

Arnold Ridley cuts the cake at his 80th birthday party.

15. THE LION HAS 'PHONES

Also appearing: Janet Davies (Mrs Pike), Bill Pertwee (ARP Warden), Avril Angers (the Telephone Operator), Timothy Carlton (Lieut. Hope Bruce), Stanley McGeagh (Sgt. Waller), Pamela Cundell, Olive Mercer, Bernadette Milnes (the Ladies in the Queue), Gilda Perry (Doreen), Linda James (Betty), Richard Jacques (Mr Cheesewright), Colin Daniel and Carson Green (the boys).

Frazer and Wilson are on patrol and witness a German bomber crash in the reservoir. When Mainwaring arrives on the scene, Walker is nowhere to be seen. Confusion is created when Jones is sent to phone GHQ. After dialling the wrong number he speaks to the cashier at the Plaza Cinema and gets confused upon hearing her say the film's title is *One Of Our Aircraft Is Missing*, and Eric Portman and Googie Withers are in it!

Back at the reservoir Hodges and Lt Hope Bruce from GHQ arrive, but it's Walker who has used his initiative. After a word with a reservoir official, the sluices are opened and the Germans swim for their lives.

BRENDA COWLING (b. London)
Role: Mrs Prentice (episode 48)

As a child, Brenda Cowling wanted to be a film star but after leaving school trained as a shorthand typist. Eventually changed direction and joined RADA (she was in the same class as Warren Mitchell and Jimmy Perry). Appeared as a drama student in Hitchcock's *Stage Fright* while still at RADA.

Plenty of rep work followed before her TV break. Early appearances include several series of an afternoon keep fit show and *The Forsyte Saga*. Her career has focused mainly on TV but seen occasionally on stage. Also appeared in films, such as *The Railway Children*, *International Velvet*, *Carry On Girls*, *Carry On Behind* and brief appearances in two Bond movies.

Post-*Dad's Army*, Brenda worked for David Croft and Jimmy Perry in *It Ain't Half Hot, Mum* as a WVS lady, and a maid in the final instalment of *Hi-De-Hi!* She played many nurses, including the Sister in an episode of *Fawlty Towers* and a matron in *Only When I Laugh*. Cast as Jane in three series of *Potter*, two of which starred Arthur Lowe.

Recent years have been dominated by four series of *You Rang, M'Lord?* in which she played Mrs Lipton. Also seen recently in *The Detectives*, *Casualty* and *The Legacy of Reginald Perrin*, as CJ's housekeeper, Mrs Wren.

ATTENTION!

'I first met Jimmy Perry in rep at Palmers Green and enjoyed working for him in *Dad's Army* as Mr Cheesewright. It was a happy period for me. The stars were kind and considerate, as were the crew. The programme is a classic and will always remain a favourite of many people around the world. I still see repeats of it in Toronto, where I've been living since 1991, and am proud to have been a small part of its success.' **RICHARD JACQUES**

16. THE BULLET IS NOT FOR FIRING

Also appearing: Janet Davies (Mrs Pike), Frank Williams (the Vicar), Tim Barrett (Capt. Pringle), Michael Knowles (Capt. Cutts), Edward Sinclair (the Verger), Harold Bennett (Mr Blewitt), May Warden (Mrs Dowding), Fred Tomlinson, Kate Forge, Eilidh McNab, Andrew Daye and Arthur Lewis (the Choir).

Trouble is in the air when the platoon blow all their ammo in a night's exercise. Mainwaring sees no alternative but to report the incident to his superiors. The gravity of the scene is punctuated by the entrance of Mrs Pike, concerned about nothing more than Frank's appearance.

MRS PIKE: Where on earth have you been? I've been worried sick about you.
PIKE: I've been shooting at aeroplanes, we think we shot one down.
MRS PIKE: 'Ere, have you washed your face?
PIKE: No, I've only just got back from shooting at aeroplanes.
MRS PIKE: Well, it's a disgrace. You're going to come straight home with me and I'll give it a good go with a flannel, come on.
PIKE: I can't, I've got to boil my rifle out.
MRS PIKE: I'll soon see about that. *(Turning to Mainwaring).* Mr Mainwaring, my Frank's coming home with me. It's a perfect disgrace you keeping him out all night like this with a dirty face.

A Court of Inquiry is held, upon Mainwaring's insistence, into the use of

Pike wasn't the safest of gun users.

75 rounds of ammo. But proceedings are farcical and peppered with constant interruptions, especially when Jones brings the ceiling down!

ATTENTION!

'The scene in this episode where John Le Mesurier walks around Mainwaring's desk saying: "Oh dear, Oh dear" all the time is brilliant. I used to watch it everyday in rehearsals because the timing is just perfect.' **FRANK WILLIAMS**

LINDA JAMES (b. Ilford)
Role: Betty (episodes 15 & 34)

On the proviso that she qualified as a teacher, Linda's parents allowed her to enrol on a drama course at The Royal Academy of Music. Three years later, she graduated as a speech and drama teacher.

Worked in rep before making her TV debut in 1969 comedy *The Gnomes of Dulwich*, written by Jimmy Perry. The series about garden gnomes meant her appearance as one of the humans was restricted to just shots of her feet! Also seen in *Keeping Up Appearances*, *Waiting for God* and *Only Fools and Horses*. In a career spanning 15 years, she was seen in mainly comedy parts.

Nowadays Linda — who's married to actor Michael Knowles — is a dialect coach for film and TV and teaches at two drama schools.

17. SOMETHING NASTY IN THE VAULT

Also appearing: Janet Davies (Mrs Pike), Bill Pertwee (ARP Warden), Norman Mitchell (Capt. Rogers), Special Guest: Robert Dorning (the Bank Inspector).

The arrival of Mr West, the bank inspector, is all Mainwaring needs. When he points out that the monthly report to head office has become irregular, Mainwaring blames the weight of responsibility, particularly as he's protecting the stretch of coastline from Stone's Amusement Arcade to the Novelty Rock Emporium. An air raid interrupts the discussion, and they return to find the bank has taken a direct hit. Both Mainwaring and Wilson fall down a gaping hole in the office and end up clutching an unexploded bomb in the bank's strongroom.

WILSON: Sir, if you could possibly lower your end just a little bit.
MAINWARING: Don't do that, the slightest movement could set this thing off.
WILSON: Well we can't sit here all day holding it like this, sir, for heaven's sake.
MAINWARING: If you don't stop jogging your end, we'll be sitting on a cloud holding a harp!

While Mainwaring and Wilson sweat buckets, Captain Rogers, bomb disposal, arrives but does little to help confidence when announcing the bomb is a trembler. While he rushes off to get the right tools, the trusty platoon members take matters into their own hands.

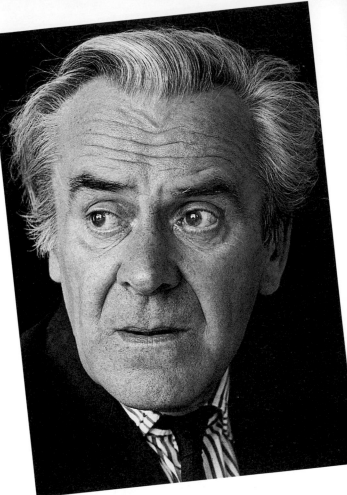

John Le Mesurier particularly enjoyed Episode 17.

ATTENTION!

'This was John's favourite episode. There are some lovely moments between him and Arthur, particularly when they're sitting holding the bomb. He had a wonderful rapport with Arthur Lowe, and loved the little moments in the episode where he was alone with him.'
JOAN LE MESURIER

18. ROOM AT THE BOTTOM

Also appearing: Anthony Sagar (Drill Sgt. Gregory), John Ringham (Cpt. Bailey), Edward Sinclair (the Verger), Colin Bean (Pte. Sponge).

When it transpires Mainwaring's self-appointment to captain isn't official, and that he hasn't even been commissioned as a lieutenant, it's demotion to private. As Wilson is put in temporary charge of the platoon, his former superior wears a brave face and attends the drill exercise.

The drill sergeant is a hard task matter. . . as Godfrey discovers:

DRILL SERGEANT: What are you laughing at then, lad?
GODFREY: I'm not really laughing, it's my normal expression.
DRILL SERGEANT: Looking at you I should think it's the only thing that is normal.

When a training exercise turns into a failure under Wilson's command, the platoon write to HQ requesting Mainwaring's reinstatement.

The platoon gets some fresh air.

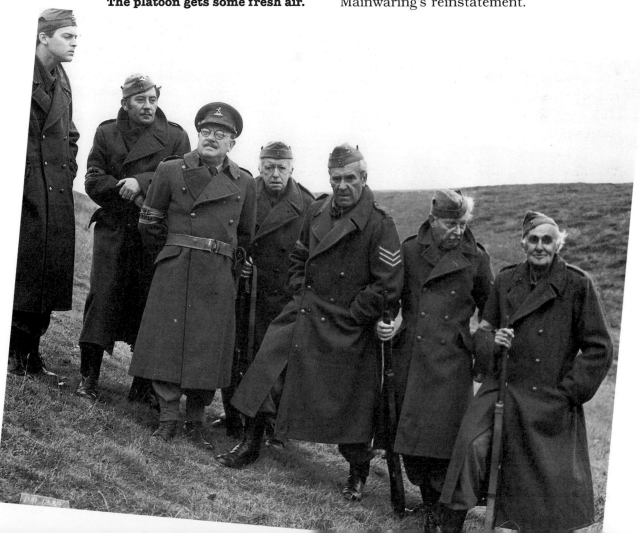

ATTENTION!

'Ann, my wife, played a big part in getting *Dad's Army* produced. She told me that Jimmy had written a comedy and encouraged him to give me the script. When it was accepted by Michael Mills, she negotiated a tough contract for him and made the BBC booker agree to the credit that has appeared ever since which reads: "Based on an idea by Jimmy Perry".'
DAVID CROFT

ATTENTION!

'I remember a few of us went to meet John Le Mesurier one evening. We decided to go for a few drinks, not a pub crawl, more of an educational trip. We got to his flat, went in and found all these Siamese cats everywhere. We couldn't sit down because they hissed at you. John said: "I'm terribly sorry, you can't sit down." So everyone stood up while the cats had all the chairs!'
DON ESTELLE

The platoon rarely had such powerful machinery.

19. BIG GUNS

Also appearing: Edward Evans (Mr Rees), Edward Sinclair (the Verger), Don Estelle (Man from Pickfords), Roy Denton (Mr Bennett).

A naval gun is delivered but Mainwaring's plans for its use in the defence of Walmington are scuppered by the town's bandstand being directly in its line of fire. He writes to the town clerk requesting its dismantling. As it's a rare example of Victorian ironwork, erected to commemorate Queen Victoria's visit in 1891, Mr Rees, the town clerk, and Mr Bennett, the borough engineer, are unhappy with Mainwaring's request. To help convince them, the platoon put on a demo of what they can do with the gun, with the usual farcical results.

20. THE DAY THE BALLOON WENT UP

Also appearing: Bill Pertwee (ARP Warden), Frank Williams (the Vicar), Edward Sinclair (the Verger), Nan Braunton (Miss Godfrey), Jennifer Browne (the WAAF Sgt.), Andrew Carr (the Operations Room Officer), Therese McMurray (the girl in the haystack), Kenneth Watson (the RAF Officer), Vicki Lane (the girl on the tandem), Harold Bennett (Mr Blewitt), Jack Haig (the Gardener).

The verger gets caught up on the cable of a barrage balloon while cleaning windows. The platoon eventually free him

Bill Pertwee and Edward Sinclair relax during a break in filming.

ATTENTION!

'Working on *Dad's Army* was a very happy period for me. The 'stars' were very kind and considerate, as were all the crew. My favourite memory is of dear old Arnold Ridley, at our lunch break when we were filming in the middle of a forest, sitting on a tree stump, eating his lunch, and looking for all the world like a little rosy gnome.' **RICHARD JACQUES**

but then have to decide what to do with the stray balloon. With help unlikely before nightfall, it's decided to take the balloon to nearby woods and tie it to a tree. As always things don't go to plan and Mainwaring is lifted in to the air, triggering a Spitfire squadron to scramble in search of an unidentified object, or is it Captain Mainwaring?

21. WAR DANCE

Also appearing: Frank Williams (the Vicar), Edward Sinclair (the Verger), Janet Davies (Mrs Pike), Nan Braunton (Miss Godfrey), Sally Douglas (Blodwen), The Graham Twins (Doris and Dora), Olive Mercer (Mrs Yeatman), Hugh Hastings (the pianist).

It's the Home Guard dance and Pikey, who's nearly 19, is bringing ATS girl Violet Gibbons, whose mother used to clean for Mainwaring. Violet worked in a fish and chip shop and Woolworth's, and Mainwaring doesn't think the girl is suitable when considering Pike's future in the bank. He persuades a chary Wilson to talk to the boy. But it's no good; Pike tells him he's announcing their engagement at the dance, even though his mother knows nothing of the relationship. At the dance,

HAROLD BENNETT (b. Hastings)
Role: Old Man (episode 13);
Mr Blewitt, also spelt Mr Bluett, (episodes 16, 20, 25, 36, 49, 53, 61, 62, 66, 70, 72, 75)

Harold's packed life resembles a colourful montage. He left school at 12 and became a jeweller's apprentice but during his lifetime he taught English during the evenings at the Working Men's College, London, studied and painted in Paris and worked as a circus clown.

After acting as an amateur he turned professional and embarked on a career involving plenty of theatre work (he toured with Donald Wolfit and made numerous West End appearances).

While his three children grew up, he took a break from the unstable acting world and worked for an electric light company, but retained his interest in acting with various amateur companies. After retiring at 65, Harold returned to acting professionally and earned the success he deserved appearing in various TV productions, among them Mr Halliforth in BBC's sitcom *Whack-O!*, but most notably as Young Mr Grace in *Are You Being Served?*

Harold, who always looked older than his age, died in 1981, aged 82, after suffering a heart attack.

Jones is told to stop Pikey getting to the mike but fails. When Mrs Pike later throws a bucket of water over Frank, he decides married life isn't for him after all.

22. MENACE FROM THE DEEP

Also appearing: Bill Pertwee (ARP Warden), Stuart Sherwin (2nd ARP Warden), Bill Treacher (1st Sailor), Larry Martyn (2nd Sailor).

The platoon are guarding the machine gun post at the end of the pier for four nights. Wilson and Mainwaring spot a hammock.

MAINWARING: Oh, I say, a hammock, good, I'll take that.
WILSON: Oh, now, really, sir.
MAINWARING: What's the matter?
WILSON: Well I really must protest, sir. Just because you're the officer you must take the hammock. I mean, you don't even say: 'May I take the hammock?' or 'Do you mind if I take the hammock?' You just strut over there, put your hand out and say: 'I'm taking that.' I mean, it's just the sort of behaviour that I cannot stand!
MAINWARING: Well I'm sorry, Wilson. Perhaps it was a little unthinking of me, a little undemocratic, but you know I'm the last person in the world to take advantage of my position.
WILSON: Oh really, sir.
MAINWARING: We shall take it in turns, of course.
WILSON: Thank you.
MAINWARING: But I shall use it first.

DICK HAYDON (b. Exeter)
Role: Raymond, Jones' assistant at the butcher's (episode 13)

Dick — in his early twenties when he appeared — was the first actor to be seen playing Raymond, Jones' young shop assistant. He was frequently referred to but hardly ever seen.

He joined the merchant navy at 16, for three years. But after visiting a London theatre in the early 1960s, he knew he wanted to become an actor and left the navy to join drama school.

His first TV job came a year later in the drama *Compact*. Subsequent years saw him busy on TV in shows such as *United!* and *Z Cars*. In the 1970s he was employed more in theatre with various West End productions.

Dick's youthful looks meant he became typecast in young roles for some time, even when he'd reached his thirties. Last worked on stage four years ago, and has been concentrating on scriptwriting ever since from his homes in England and France.

In *Branded* Godfrey is installed as medical orderly.

During their stay on the pier, Pikey fails to secure the rowing boat and it drifts out to sea taking the tangled telephone wire with it; and they have to deal with a wandering sea mine.

23. BRANDED

Also appearing: Bill Pertwee (Chief Warden), Nan Braunton (Miss Godfrey), Stuart Sherwin (2nd ARP Warden), Roger Avon (the Doctor).

Godfrey hands in his notice. When interviewed by Mainwaring, he confesses to having been a conscientious objector during the last campaign. He's sent home in disgrace while Mainwaring informs the rest of the platoon, who cold shoulder the old man. But when Mainwaring passes out during an exercise in a smoke-filled room, it's Godfrey who comes to the rescue, saving the captain's life. While Godfrey's recovering from his ordeal, he's visited by the platoon. Spotting a photo of Godfrey wearing the Military Medal, apologies follow and Godfrey is installed as the platoon's medical orderly.

24. MAN HUNT

Also appearing: Bill Pertwee (Chief Warden), Janet Davies (Mrs Pike), Patrick Tull (the Suspect), Robert Moore (the Large Man), Leon Cortez (the Small Man), Olive Mercer (the Fierce Lady), Miranda Hampton (Sexy lady), Bran (himself), Robert Aldous (German pilot).

'I was employed to play a German pilot in *Christmas Night With The Stars* in 1969, which was recorded in tandem with this episode. Jimmy and David didn't feel the end of *Man Hunt* tied up very well, so asked whether I'd rush on at the end, again as a pilot, and say one line. I wasn't to tell the rest of the cast, just to come on at the technical rehearsal. When I did it the rest of the cast stared as if I was stark raving bonkers. It was an interesting episode to work on because normally when you rehearse a TV show, people that aren't required sit and read newspapers. But on *Dad's Army* people moved between sets watching each other because the comedy was so inventive, and no one wanted to miss anything.'

ROBERT ALDOUS

ARNOLD DIAMOND (b. London)
Role: Major-General Anstruther Stephenson (episode 73)

Arnold, whose character had the misfortune to experience Mainwaring's inebriated brother Barry at a church hall function, started his working life as a librarian, acting as an amateur during the evenings.

During the war he was wounded and taken to an Italian hospital for POWs. Whilst there he wrote and directed plays for fellow prisoners. After demob he decided to try it professionally and studied at RADA.

Many years in rep followed before his TV career began to dominate. He appeared in *The Borgias*, *Citizen Smith*, and *Master Spy*. His final appearance in a series was *In Sickness and in Health*. Among his 60-plus films are favourites such as: *The Italian Job*, *The Constant Husband*, *Carry On Sergeant* (as the fifth specialist treating Kenneth Connor) and *Zeppelin*.

Although most of his roles were small, his services were in demand in every aspect of the entertainment business, including theatre and radio, particularly playing suave official types.

Arnold died in 1992.

Walker introduces a tracking dog to the platoon, and as the canine recruit lollops across the floor, Mainwaring decides to test it out against Jones. When a discarded parachute is discovered in the area, the dog is put to work and is successful in tracking down an ornithologist, after a rare bird's egg.

25. NO SPRING FOR FRAZER
Also appearing: Frank Williams (the Vicar), Edward Sinclair (the Verger), Harold Bennett (Mr Blewitt), Joan Cooper (Miss Baker), Ronnie Brandon (Mr Drury).

Mainwaring orders Wilson to march the platoon over to the rec for the field craft lecture, and asks his sergeant whether he obtained appropriate permission.

WILSON: Oh yes, he would like us to keep away from the children's swings and the Donald Duck sandpit.
MAINWARING: He'll soon change his tune when he hears the tramp, tramp of Nazi jackboots pounding over his bowling greens.

When Mainwaring inspects the Lewis gun Frazer has been looking after he notices the butterfly spring missing. En route to the rec they pop into Frazer's workshop but discover the spring fell into the coffin of the recently deceased Horace Blewitt, brother of Sidney, in whose house he lies in rest. The platoon head for 21 Marigold

GORDON PETERS (b. Co. Durham)
Role: The Soldier (episode 3); Policeman (episode 11); Lighthouse Keeper (episode 33); Man with the Door (episode 69).

A chorister at Durham Cathedral for six years, Gordon worked for Standard Bank as a bank clerk, and emigrated to Southern Rhodesia with the job. Whilst there he rekindled his interest in acting, winning a talent contest in the process.

Returned to the UK at 25 and kicked off his acting career. Worked mainly as a stand-up comic until club work became scarce. *Dad's Army* was the first of many TV parts alongside his role as a warm-up artist. Also appeared in *Now Take My Wife* and a series of his own show *The Gordon Peters Show*. Recent work includes cameos in *Keeping Up Appearances* and *One Foot in the Grave*.

Lately, Gordon has been doing a lot of old-time music hall acts around the country.

Avenue during the night in an attempt to recover the spring only to find the coffin lid has been screwed down. At the funeral, Mainwaring and his men put Plan B into action: they cause the ceremony to be abandoned by suggesting there is an unexploded bomb in the area. Further attempts to retrieve the spring fail before Frazer suddenly comes across it in his pocket.

down their 50th Nazi plane for the enemy. Hiding in a railway wagon overnight, they wake to find themselves travelling through the countryside. They make plans to cross enemy territory when the train stops at . . . Eastbourne Station!

26. SONS OF THE SEA

Also appearing: Michael Bilton (Mr Maxwell), Ralph Ball (Man on Station), John Leeson (the 1st Soldier), Jonathan Holt (the 2nd Soldier).

Mainwaring and his men take possession of the late Mr Johnson's boat *The Naughty Jane* which they put to use as a patrol boat. The platoon are in trouble when they get lost in the fog, drifting aimlessly in the English Channel. When they reach land, they confuse the sound of the nearby party being thrown by the French Canadians celebrating shooting

CORPORAL JONES

Corporal Jack 'They don't like it up 'em!' Jones is a vital cog in Walmington's local defence machine. Although his age is taking its toll physically, he's always a second behind in drill, Jones is a lionheart – always faithful to the cause and the man Mainwaring needs to help knock the platoon into shape.

Rightly proud of his distinguished war record, Jones spent 30 years in the army, during which he served in the Sudan, under General Kitchener. In the Great War he saw action in France.

When the war years were over, Jones followed in his father's footsteps and opened a butcher's shop in Walmington. Always keen to do the best for his clients, he's prone to providing a little 'under the counter' oxtail or sausages to the favoured few, particularly Mainwaring or Mrs Fox, his longtime sweetheart, whom he later wed.

To a man who has spent most of his acting career playing old men, the part of Corporal Jones must have been right up Clive Dunn's street. 'I always played older characters but didn't mind because it always seemed to work,' he admits.

'You put the right hat on, the right moustache, have the right attitude and just dive in and hope for the best. With Jones everything clicked. I

knew the character, somehow. In my mind I was clear about how he should act – it must have been instinct.

'Playing Jones was certainly my cup of tea and knowing David Croft, an old friend, wanted me for the part was pleasing.'

Clive Dunn quickly settled into the role of Walmington's panicky butcher, stamping his own style on the part. He was appreciative of Jimmy Perry and David Croft's ability to fine-tune the roles to exploit an actor's idiosyncrasies. 'As the weeks went by, they realised what we all did best and made use of it; this is why each character seemed so strong on screen.'

It's abundantly clear that Clive enjoyed appearing in *Dad's Army,* so why did he take so long before agreeing to play the old-timer? 'John Le Mesurier was the key, really. Once I knew he'd decided to play Wilson, I accepted my offer. We kept speaking about the show and I think we must have been waiting for each other to decide,' he explains.

'By this time David Croft and Jimmy Perry were getting fed up waiting for my decision because they wanted to get on with the series. But John Le Mesurier was the only one I knew in the cast, so I was keen to know whether he was going to be in it.

'And, of course, there had already been *The Army Game*, and I was a little worried that another series about the army might be too soon – it depended entirely on how the series was going to be done. Obviously I was keen to work, but still felt unsure about the idea after I'd accepted.'

When Clive discovered Le Mesurier wasn't playing the officer, as one might expect, but the sergeant, he was confident the show was full of promise and any initial doubts were dispelled. 'The idea of a sophisticated performer like John playing the sergeant was such a different approach, it put the stamp on it for me,' he says.

When the first series was transmitted back in 1968, Clive knew the programme stood a good chance of success. 'Despite it being shown at a poor time of year, in the summer when everyone is on holiday, it still worked well enough for a second series to be commissioned.'

Born in London in 1920, Clive made his professional stage debut over 60 years ago – first as a dancing frog, then as a flying dragon at the Holborn Empire. Both his parents were in the entertainment business, so it came as no surprise when their son entered the profession at the age of 16.

But no sooner had he begun his thespian life than war broke out. Serving with the 4th Hussars, he spent four years as a POW in

Austria. 'That's where my great passion for drawing started,' he explains. 'All prisoners were locked in from midday on the Saturday until the Monday morning so you had to do something to pass the time. With all the people sat around me I began drawing portraits; after all they were captive models!

'I gave it up after the war because acting took

Theatre during the war years and remembers Clive's time at the theatre, partly for his style of humour. 'I think he used his performances there as a training ground for his particular sort of humour. He did monologues, just talking about nothing really, but being very funny.

'When I watch *Dad's Army* I'm convinced he was allowed to do a little ad-libbing as Jones because it's very much the type of humour he was successful with at The Players.'

Nowadays Clive lives in Portugal with his wife, actress Priscilla Morgan. 'We spent most of our careers trying to earn enough money to have regular holidays here,' he explains, 'then realised we would like to end up living here some day.

'We bought our current place as a holiday home about 19 years ago. I tried retiring about ten years ago but found myself constantly returning to England to do the odd piece of work. Now I am supposed to be fully retired but I still find plenty of things to do.'

Dad's Army isn't shown in Portugal, but a week doesn't pass without more fan letters dropping through the letter box. 'I'll always be eternally grateful to Jimmy Perry and David Croft for not just giving me the chance to be in the series, but of taking care of it so well.'

over, but I'm pleased to have resumed my interest in drawing, painting and sculpting now that I have more time to myself.'

After demob, Clive returned to the stage and spent many years working in theatres and music halls before becoming a household name playing Old Johnson in *Bootsie and Snudge* in the early-1960s. Other small screen successes have included numerous roles in *It's A Square World*, with Michael Bentine, and his own series, *My Old Man*. He also played Charlie Quick in the 1970s children's show *Grandad*.

Veteran actress Jean Anderson, an ardent *Dad's Army* fan, helped run London's Players

ROSEMARY FAITH (b. Belfast)
Role: Ivy Samways (episode 35);
Barmaid (episode 40);
Waitress (episode 64)

Diminutive Rosemary Faith first worked for David Croft in BBC's *Beggar My Neighbour* in 1967 as the daughter of Rose Garvey (played by June Whitfield). A stage engagement in *Gypsy* meant she was unavailable when Ivy reappeared (episode 55), so the part went to Ian Lavender's then wife, Suzanne Kerchiss.

At 17, Rosemary attended the Webber Douglas Academy. In the audience of the Press Show at graduation was David Croft. While working as ASM in Coventry she met David's wife who, realising Rosemary wanted to break into TV, suggested she wrote to David. Eight months David offered her a part in *Beggar My Neighbour*, initially playing a hairdresser's assistant.

Worked in rep and the West End throughout her career. Also toured with Clive Dunn in *The Chiltern Hundreds*. On TV appeared in the drama series *People Like Us*, *Oppenheimer*, the last 12 episodes of *Please, Sir!* and also popped up in *The Goodies*.

Went back to Northern Ireland for a spell in the late 1980s, and upon returning in 1988 decided to give up acting. Now involved in theatre administration in Worthing.

CROFT ON DUNN

Rehearsals for *Dad's Army* took place at first in various church halls and later in the BBC's rehearsal room complex in North Acton. The doors of the set were marked by moveable metal poles and the walls by white tape stuck to the floor. All the actors got on quite well with this arrangement except for Clive Dunn, who consistently went from Mainwaring's office to the church hall by crossing the white line. One day Jimmy Perry could stand it no more. 'Do you realise,' said Jimmy, 'that you keep on walking through the office wall?' To which Clive replied witheringly: 'Well, I won't be able to do it on the set when the wall is actually there, will I?'

Jones stands by his beloved, Mrs Fox.

JOHN LAURIE

When he's not playing soldiers in Walmington's Home Guard, the peppery James Frazer is the local undertaker. Assisted by Heathcliff, he works in his high street shop sandwiched between Jones' butcher's shop and Hodges' greengrocery.

Born on the Isle of Barra, Frazer learnt how to fish and make coffins as a boy, placing him in good stead for his move to Walmington after sailing the high seas. During the Great War, he was a naval cook, serving at the Battle of Jutland.

Now, the President and sole member of the town's Caledonian Society, Frazer isn't one of life's instantly likeable characters. A great cynic, he spreads gloom wherever he goes. With his wild, staring eyes, he's forever deriding Mainwaring's plans, spouting: 'We're doomed!' If that wasn't enough, he's also prone to excessive bouts of creating rumours.

When the chance to play Frazer came John Laurie's way, he accepted it with little enthusiasm. 'He never turned work down,' explains his daughter, Veronica, 'but he certainly wasn't enthused by the idea.' This caused difficulties when the BBC commissioned a second series and he was asked to step back into the fiery Scotsman's shoes. 'I remember he didn't want to play the character again, it took

some persuading by David Croft, Jimmy Perry and his agent to change his mind.' Fortunately for everyone, he did.

During *Dad's Army,* John formed a strong friendship with Ian Lavender, who grew very fond of the Scottish actor. 'John could be acerbic with anyone, regardless as to whether he liked you or not – but that was his style. We got on from day one, probably because I was the youngest and he was one of the oldest in the platoon.

'Often I'd drive him home. I remember driving from Brighton, where we'd been filming. As we got to the outskirts of Brighton, he asked whether I'd like him to recite something. I jumped at the offer, and from there to London he gave a splendid solo performance of *Tam O'Shanter.*'

Ian also recalls the friendly rivalry that existed between John and fellow veteran, Arnold Ridley. 'There was always a sense of competition between John and Arnold, being the oldest members of the cast.

'At the start of location filming once, Arnold arrived in a big limo; he'd broken his hip and with a leg in plaster stuck out in front of him, he needed plenty of leg room. We all went out to greet him, except John. When he did finally go over, David Croft was leaning into the car shaking his hand. From a distance all John could see was David leaning towards Arnold, with his

arm going up and down. John turned to me and said: "Look, they're pumping him up! They're pumping him up!" It wasn't meant nastily, it was just a little victory for John that he didn't need the same treatment!'

Born in Dumfries in 1897, John's upbringing was tough. His father – who was a foreman of a mill before opening his own gentlemen's outfitters – died when John was only three. He won a scholarship to the Dumfries Academy, before taking up an apprenticeship in a local architect's office. 'He began as an articled clerk earning £5 a year,' says Veronica Laurie. 'He worked there until he joined up.'

During the Great War he served with the Honourable Artillery Company and fought at the Somme. Invalided out due to bronchial problems, he finished his war service in London. John never talked in detail about his past, particularly the war years. 'Either people talk and rid themselves of the horrors that way, or just shut the memories away, and my father fell into the latter category,' says Veronica. ' For him, the trench warfare was so horrific he'd never speak about it.'

Back in civvy street, John needed a job quickly. Deciding he couldn't afford to return to his apprenticeship in the architect's office, he turned his mind to acting. Upon joining a local dramatic society he soon discovered he possessed a talent for the stage and that people enjoyed listening to him.

While attending a two-week summer school at Stratford-upon-Avon run by Elsie Fogerty, he was persuaded to take up acting professionally.

John Laurie displays his Scottish roots.

JANET DAVIES (b. Wakefield)
Role: Mrs Mavis Pike (30 episodes)

Janet's father, a solicitor, died in his early thirties, and as a result she was sent to boarding school. Deciding not to train as a solicitor, she qualified as a shorthand typist and worked for the BBC before moving into rep in 1948.

Worked in various reps at Leatherhead, Watford and Northampton while early TV work included several episodes of *Dixon of Dock Green* and *Z Cars*.

Also made a few films: *Under Milk Wood* with Richard Burton, *The Hiding Place*, *In This House of Brede* and *Something in Disguise*.

Other TV work included a librarian in *The Last of the Summer Wine*, *The Professionals*, *General Hospital*, *The Fall and Rise of Reginald Perrin* and *All Creatures Great and Small*.

When she wasn't acting, Janet exploited her typing and shorthand training by working with various theatrical agencies.

A true jobbing actress she kept busy throughout her career, but will always be remembered as Mrs Pike. She died of cancer in 1986, aged 56.

His early theatrical career was heavily focused on Shakespeare and he established a reputation as an adept classical actor. 'My father had studied Shakespeare, and admired and loved his work,' says Veronica. 'He also enjoyed verse and was a proponent of verse-speaking.' John served in the Home Guard during the Second World War, by which time he'd become leading man at Stratford, playing the likes of Hamlet, Macbeth Othello and Richard III.

His film career had also taken off with appearances in over a dozen films, including: Hitchcock's *Juno and the Paycock*, *The 39 Steps* and the Gainsborough picture, *The Tudor Rose*.

The cessation of hostilities in 1945 marked a significant juncture in John's professional life. He resumed his big screen career with ease but his stage career never returned to the heights it

JONATHAN CECIL (b. London)
Role: Captain Cadbury (episode 59)

Jonathan played loopy Captain Cadbury who talked to his dogs as if they were a platoon. He became involved in acting at Oxford. After a university performance at Stratford he was told he had a future in the profession, so upon graduating joined LAMDA.

Rep work followed before Jonathan moved into TV. Early screen credits include snooty Jeremy Crichton-Jones in two series of *Romany Jones*, Ben Travers' Farces, *The Goodies* and *Dick Emery Show*. As well as an extensive TV career, Jonathan has made over 20 film appearances, including *Rising Damp*, *The Yellow Rolls Royce*, *Up the Front* and *Alice Through the Looking Glass*.

Jonathan's busy career has graced all areas of the profession, and he remains busy today.

had reached during the 1930s. 'As theatres reopened after the war there was a whole draft of new actors who'd grown in stature,' says Veronica.

One could have expected John Laurie to be frustrated by this, but as Veronica points out: 'He was a man who accepted life as it was, never looking back with regret. This was a quality I admired in him.'

During a career spanning six decades, John made nearly 100 films, including such classics as: *Trio, Fanny By Gaslight, Rockets Galore!* and the 1979 production, *The Prisoner of Zenda*. With his pronounced facial features, bushy brows and wild-eyed expressions, he was often cast as irascible eccentrics.

Although the financial rewards were greater, John wasn't impressed with many of the pictures he appeared in. He admitted that ninety-nine per cent of them were instantly forgettable, and that he wouldn't want to see them again.

Very much a homebird, John was a private man who enjoyed nothing more than relaxing with a good book or completing *The Times'* crossword. He died of emphysema in 1980. A septuagenarian by the time *Dad's Army* started in 1968, John had reached the twilight of his career. Despite his initial reservations, he was grateful for the work at this late age, regarding it to be 'the finest pension an old man could have.'

PERRY ON LAURIE

John was a highly educated man and a serious Shakespearean scholar. He was also totally mad. He had complete disdain for 'semi-literate Sassenachs' as he called me. Nevertheless, we got on amazingly well and became very close.

TALFRYN THOMAS (b. Swansea)
Role: Mr Cheeseman (episodes 55 & 62); Private Cheeseman (episodes 63, 64, 65, 66)

Son of a butcher, Talfryn grew up in Swansea and upon leaving school trained as an instrument mechanic, working in the local weights and measures office until war broke out.

As a sideline, he joined the Landore Players, a local amateur dramatic society, but he didn't pursue acting professionally until after serving in the RAF during the Second World War.

Having returned to his role as an instrument mechanic, he then decided to make acting his career. Trained at RADA and after success in provincial theatre moved into TV, playing roles such as Tom Price in BBC's sci-fi series, *Survivors* as well as appearing in *Coronation Street*. Also teamed up with Ken Dodd for numerous radio and TV shows.

Appeared in a handful of films, including Mr Pugh in *Under Milk Wood*. His character in *Dad's Army* became a regular for the seventh season after Jimmy Beck's death.

His last TV appearance was in *Hi-De-Hi!* Talfryn died in 1982, aged 60, after a heart attack.

John often played eccentrics.

Series Guide: SEASONS 4-5

SEASON FOUR

Transmitted 25/9/70 – 18/12/70

27. THE BIG PARADE

Also appearing: Bill Pertwee (ARP Warden), Janet Davies (Mrs Pike), Edward Sinclair (the Verger), Colin Bean (Private Sponge), Pamela Cundell (Mrs Fox).

Mainwaring decides the platoon needs a mascot, particularly as on Sunday morning they will be leading the big parade to mark the start of Spitfire Week. Private Sponge donates a ram – if anyone can catch one at his farm. During the chase at Sponge's farm, Wilson gets caught on barbed wire and Pikey falls in a bog. After several failed attempts, the boy is finally rescued. The parade takes place without the mascot, even though Walker offered a goat as an alternative.

ATTENTION!

'The Big Parade was a very uncomfortable episode because I spent most of my time stuck in a bog. A hole was filled with water, then topped with earth and cork. I stood on a set of steps and gradually stepped down so it looked as if I was sinking deeper into the bog. It was deemed a waste of time to get out for tea breaks, so drinks – deliberately laced with liquor for warmth – were handed out on a tray nailed to a long piece of wood. Other than getting out for lunch, I was in the bog all day in my wet suit.' **IAN LAVENDER**

28. DON'T FORGET THE DIVER

Also appearing: Bill Pertwee (ARP Warden), Edward Sinclair (the Verger), Frank Williams (the Vicar), Geoffrey Lumsden (Capt. Square), Robert Raglan (the H.G. Sergeant), Colin Bean (Private Sponge), Don Estelle (2nd ARP Warden), Verne Morgan (the Landlord).

A big exercise takes place between all the Home Guard units and the Walmington platoon have to plant a bomb in the windmill occupied by the Eastgate mob. Mainwaring and his team use various forms of disguise to reach the windmill unnoticed, even though the Verger is spying for Captain Square. After negotiating a chasing dog, Jones throws

Jones negotiates the windmill.

the bomb into the windmill but gets caught up on the mill's sails. As Mainwaring confronts Square and demands his surrender, the platoon can pat themselves on the back for a well-executed plan.

29. BOOTS, BOOTS, BOOTS

Also appearing: Bill Pertwee (ARP Warden), Janet Davies (Mrs Pike), Erik Chitty (Mr Sedgewick).

Mainwaring introduces the three Fs: fast feet, functional feet and fit feet. After inspecting the men's feet he announces a series of route marches. After a seven-mile trek he plans to inspect their feet again, but takes Wilson into the office to check his in private, to save embarrassment.

WILSON: Yes, quite, in that case who's going to inspect your feet, sir?
MAINWARING: (Rubbing his chin) Yes, I see your point. Look here. (He moves closer to Wilson) You show me yours and I'll show you mine.

The platoon feel Mainwaring is getting obsessed by this drive for healthy feet, particularly when he organises a barefoot football match, running across the pebbled beach and marching in the sea. But when he announces the 20-mile route march, that's the final straw. The platoon plan swapping Mainwaring's boots with a smaller pair in an attempt to make his feet hurt and prevent him completing the march. But they hadn't accounted for the shopkeeper returning another pair of Mainwaring's boots from repair just in time for the march.

30. SGT. – SAVE MY BOY!

Also appearing: Bill Pertwee (ARP Warden), Janet Davies (Mrs Pike), Michael Knowles (Engineer Officer).

The platoon take over the Harris Orphans' Holiday Home Hut on the beach and Pikey gets caught on barbed wire in the middle of a mine field. While they await the arrival of the Engineers to clear a path, Mainwaring checks progress.

MAINWARING: What news of the sappers, Wilson?
WILSON: I'm just on to them now, sir . . . yes, it really is most terribly kind of you, but I wonder if you could possibly manage to get here just a teeny-weeny bit sooner, we really would be most awfully grateful – thank you so much, it's so kind of you, alright, goodbye.

MAINWARING: *(Fed up with Wilson's approach)* Well?
WILSON: They're having trouble with a land mine, sir, I think. They'll be about three hours I'm afraid.

As Pikey can't swim and the tide is rushing in, there's no alternative but for the platoon to rescue their comrade. As the men progress cautiously across the sand, Godfrey reaches Pike from another angle, much to Mainwaring's surprise.

31. DON'T FENCE ME IN

Also appearing: Edward Evans (General Monteverdi), John Ringham (Capt. Bailey), Larry Martyn (Italian POW).

For two weekends, the platoon are responsible for guarding Italian POWs. There is a shortage of discipline which irks Mainwaring: prisoners are listening to music and generally idling. In the evening, Walker meets up with the Italian general and discusses plans for getting them out of the camp; Godfrey overhears and reports back to Mainwaring, who suspects Joe of being a fifth columnist. They catch him red-handed, loading prisoners into the platoon van. Walker confesses to employing them on night shift helping to assemble radio parts. When Captain Bailey (GHQ) arrives to inspect the prisoners, panic breaks out.

32. ABSENT FRIENDS

Also appearing: Bill Pertwee (ARP Warden), Janet Davies (Mrs Pike), Edward Sinclair

ATTENTION!

'I'd worked with Jimmy Perry at Watford Rep during the 1950s. I hadn't spoken to him for years when he called out of the blue, saying: "You know that mad Italian waiter you played at Watford, well you'll be just right for a part I've written called General Monteverdi." He asked whether I was interested and I told him whenever money is concerned, I'm interested. It was a very funny part and I enjoyed playing him.'
EDWARD EVANS

(the Verger), J.G. Devlin (Regan), Arthur English (the Policeman), Patrick Connor (Shamus), Verne Morgan (the Landlord), Michael Lomax (2nd ARP Warden).

When Mainwaring has a meeting cancelled, he turns up at the church hall to find Wilson has given the men permission to play darts in the local pub against the ARP wardens. Mainwaring is

ROBERT DORNING (b. St Helens)
Role: Bank Inspector (episode 17)

Robert trained as a ballet dancer before turning to musical comedy prior to the war. Following demob from the RAF, he resumed his career in musical comedies and increasingly moved into acting.

Worked for three years with Arthur Lowe in Granada's *Pardon the Expression* (they had previously worked together in *Coronation Street*) playing Walter Hunt. A well-known face on TV, he also spent four years in *Bootsie and Snudge* between 1960 and 1964, with Clive Dunn.

Made over 25 films including *They Came By Night, Man Accused*, and *The Black Windmill*. He played the Prime Minister in *Carry On Emmanuelle*.

Robert's career encompassed all facets of the entertainment world. He died in 1989.

furious and orders Wilson to get everyone back in ten minutes – but as there are two pints for the victors of the match, no one is prepared to leave. Mainwaring cannot believe the men are acting this way and finds himself short of help when an armed IRA suspect is reported at 27 Ivy Crescent.

33. PUT THAT LIGHT OUT

Also appearing: Bill Pertwee (ARP Warden), Stuart Sherwin (the 2nd ARP Warden), Gordon Peters (the Lighthouse Keeper), Avril Angers (the Telephone Operator).

Mainwaring sets up an observation post in a lighthouse and Jones' section are first on duty. By accident they switch on the light, illuminating the whole of Walmington just as the siren warns of approaching enemy bombers. As the lighthouse has its own generator, it's vital that Mainwaring gets a message to Jones – the trouble is the phone is disconnected. His attempts to get the line reconnected via the exchange are fruitless until Walker takes control.

WALKER: *(Speaking to Mainwaring)* Come here, give it to me will you. *(He takes the phone).* 'Ello Freda.
OPERATOR: Who's that?
WALKER: It's Joe, Joe Walker.
OPERATOR: Oh! *(Smiling and tidying her hair)* Hello, Joe.
WALKER: 'Ere, listen luv, stick 73 into 21 will you?
OPERATOR: Oh, Joe, what you up to

now? Alright then, I'll do it for you. Hang on. *(She reconnects the line)*
WALKER: 'Ere you are, sir, she's putting you through. *(Hands the phone back to Mainwaring)*
MAINWARING: You seem very well informed.
WALKER: Well we used to run the brandy from France before the war in the motor boats, you know. And there was this bent coastguard who used to give us a tip-off when they were coming round the bay.

Mainwaring is finally able to instruct Jones how to turn the light off just before enemy planes pass overhead.

34. THE TWO AND A HALF FEATHERS

Also appearing: Bill Pertwee (the ARP Warden), John Cater (Private Clarke), Wendy Richard (Edith), Queenie Watts (Edna), Gilda Perry (Doreen), Linda James

A scene from _The Two And A Half Feathers_.

HANA-MARIA PRAVDA
(b. Prague)
Role: Interpreter (episode 58)

Hana-Maria believes she resembled a young Maggie Thatcher wearing a strange hat in her role as the fiery interpreter accompanying a Russian visitor.

She grew up in Czechoslovakia and during the Second World War was held in a German concentration camp. As soon as hostilities ended, Hana-Maria returned to the stage and resumed her acting career.

Had already established herself as an actress in Czechoslovakia (three leading film roles and experience at the country's National Theatre) when she left for Australia. Ran her own theatre company in Melbourne for six years before being spotted by Sybil Thorndike who invited her back to London.

Shortly after arriving, Hana-Maria was cast in a TV series with child actress Mandy Miller. Many theatre roles followed. Recent stage work has included a spell at The Globe Theatre with Tom Conti, and Agatha Christie's Poirot and playing Mrs Emma Cohen in BBC's Survivors on TV.

Lately, has been working in radio. Her war diaries, written during her time in the concentration camp, will be broadcast shortly.

JOAN COOPER (b. Chesterfield)
Role: Miss Baker (episode 25); Miss Fortescue (episode 53); Dolly (episodes 69, 74 & 80)

Joan's parents were musicians and although she learnt to play the piano, her inclinations veered towards another strand of the entertainment world: the stage. And so she joined the Stratford-upon-Avon Dramatic School.

Her professional career began at the age of 17, working for Donald Wolfit. Later joined Colchester Rep where she became stage manager while acting in various small roles. Theatre was the mainstay of her career, but she made various TV appearances, including BBC's Rookery Nook in 1970, Mrs Marriott in 1985's Don't Wait Up and three separate roles in Dad's Army, most notably as Dolly, one of Private Godfrey's ancient sisters.

She made appearances in several films including: Sweet William, The Bawdy Adventures of Tom Jones and The Ruling Class.

Joan, who was married to Arthur Lowe, never recovered from the shock of losing her husband in 1982. She died in 1987.

ATTENTION!

'My character, Betty, had a nice little double-act with Doreen, played by Gilda Perry. We served food at the British Restaurant in this episode and worked in the cinema box office in The Lion Has 'Phones. I just wish the two characters could have appeared more. Snoek was on the menu in this episode, and I remember my mother talking about it. She took me to a British Restaurant when I was a kid – the food was awful.' **LINDA JAMES**

(Betty), Parnell McGarry (Elizabeth), John Ash (Raymond).

George Clarke, a former colleague of Jones' in the Sudan, arrives in town and joins the platoon. It's not long before the new face begins tarnishing the butcher's war record, claiming Jones left him in the desert to die. The morning post brings Jones three anonymous letters and the stark message that there's no room in Walmington for a coward! It's time for action. After Clarke recalls his version of events to Mainwaring, Jones presents his side of the story, stating that he and Clarke were captured in the desert but that he overcame one of the captors and rescued an unconscious Clarke who'd been pegged down in the blazing heat to die. A disgraced Clarke scuttles off to the station and Jones' military reputation remains intact.

ATTENTION!

'Occasionally I'd drive John Laurie home after rehearsals. One day we were held up at a road block when a policeman came over and started questioning where I was going. Suddenly spotting John sat in the back, he jumped to a salute and told me to carry on – I couldn't believe it!'
EVAN ROSS

35. MUM'S ARMY

Also appearing: Carmen Silvera (Mrs Gray), Janet Davies (Mrs Pike), Wendy Richard (Edith Parish), Pamela Cundell (Mrs Fox), Julian Burberry (Miss Ironside), Rosemary Faith (Ivy Samways), Melita Manger (the Waitress), David Gilchrist (the Serviceman), Eleanor Smale (Mrs Prosser), Deirdre Costello (the Buffet Attendant), Jack Le White (the Porter).

The womenfolk want to join Mainwaring in the war effort. New recruits include Mrs Fox; the timorous Ivy Samways from Jutland Drive; usherette Edith Parish and Fiona Gray who recently moved from London with her mother, to whom Mainwaring takes an instant shine. On parade he puts the women through their paces, while perpetually complimenting Mrs Gray.

   After Mainwaring meets Mrs Gray at Ann's Pantry the next day, rumours spread that there is more to this relationship than meets the eye.

   At the next parade Mrs Gray's absence is explained when Ivy reports seeing her

heading for the station. Mainwaring gives chase and spots her in the station buffet. Upon learning she's returning to London, he opens his heart.

MAINWARING: But . . . but I don't want you to go. The whole pattern of my life has changed. I just live from one meeting to the next.
MRS GRAY: I know, and I'm just the same but it's the only thing to do – people are talking.
MAINWARING: People always talk, who cares about that?
MRS GRAY: But there's your wife.
MAINWARING: No one will talk to her. She hasn't left the house since Munich!
MRS GRAY: Be sensible, George. You can't afford scandal and tittle-tattle.
MAINWARING: I tell you, I don't care.
MRS GRAY: But there's the bank.
MAINWARING: Damn the bloody bank!

Mainwaring implores her to stay but she goes, leaving Mainwaring with a broken heart.

36. THE TEST

Also appearing: Bill Pertwee (the ARP Warden), Frank Williams (the Vicar), Edward Sinclair (the Verger), Don Estelle (Gerald), Harold Bennett (Mr Blewitt), Freddie Trueman (special appearance as E. C. Egan.).

Hodges challenges the platoon to a cricket match. Mainwaring selects himself as captain and proceeds to give the men some advice on batting stances until he

Freddie Trueman (far right) made a guest appearance in *The Test*.

gets bowled first ball by Pike. Jones arrives late.

JONES: I'm sorry I'm late, Mr Mainwaring – I did the coupon counting and then the sausages arrived.
MAINWARING: I don't want any excuses, Jones. A parade is a parade, you should be on time you know.
JONES: Yes, I've put your pound of sausages in the right-hand drawer of your desk as usual.
MAINWARING: *(Feeling embarrassed)* Thank you, Jones. Just watch it in future.

Hodges has a secret weapon in his team: the cricket pro Ernie Egan, who signs on as a warden to cover him for playing. With the verger and vicar as umpires, Hodges' team bat first, clocking up a total of 152 for 4 declared, with 24 being taken off one ball. There is much tension during the match and Mainwaring nearly gets his marching orders after an altercation with the verger about a no-ball.

MAINWARING: That was my googly.
VERGER: From where I was standing it looked like a chuck, and don't argue with

ATTENTION!

'I was annoyed with David Croft in *The Test* because he wouldn't let me keep wicket for Freddie Trueman, who made a special appearance in the episode. He was my boyhood hero and all I wanted to do was take a few balls from him. I pleaded with David, but to no avail. In my studio-based scene I had to bowl Arthur Lowe first ball – and I did.' **IAN LAVENDER**

the umpire or you'll be sent off.
MAINWARING: You don't send people off in cricket!
VERGER: I do!
MAINWARING: I suppose I'm lucky not to be given offside!
VERGER: I'm taking your name for that.

With three hours to go, Mainwaring's team make heavy weather of reaching the target even though Mr Egan strains his shoulder bowling. As the wickets tumble, Wilson is the saviour with a glorious innings, but it's Godfrey who shocks even himself when he scores the winning runs with a six!

37. A. WILSON (MANAGER)?
Also appearing: Frank Williams (the Vicar), Edward Sinclair (the Verger), Janet Davies (Mrs Pike), Blake Butler (Mr West), Robert Raglan (Capt. Pritchard), Arthur Brough (Mr Boyle), Colin Bean (Private Sponge), Hugh Hastings (Private Hastings).

It's a bad morning for Mainwaring: Wilson's promoted to manager at the Eastgate branch and his commission comes through. Hastily, Mainwaring appoints Pike as relief Chief Clerk and Jones as sergeant of the platoon – that is until there's a mix-up with a memo sent to all members of the platoon confirming their promotion to sergeant! Fortunately the mess sorts itself out when Wilson's dream of being manager is shattered when the bank takes a direct hit during a bombing raid. He returns to his subservient role at the Walmington branch.

RONNIE BRODY (b. Bristol)
Role: Bob (episode 56);
Mr Swann (episode 71);
GPO Man (episode 79)

Son of music hall artistes Bourne and Lester, Ronnie joined the merchant navy at 15 before serving with the RAF in North Africa during the Second World War.

After demob spent several years in Variety and rep but by the 1950s his career was dominated by both the big and small screen. Over the years became one of the most instantly recognisable comedy character actors in the business.

During his career he worked with many top comedians in shows such as *Dave Allen At Large, The Dick Emery Show, Rising Damp, Bless This House, Home James, The Lenny Henry Show* and *The 19th Hole*. He was seen in films such as *Help!, A Funny Thing Happened on the Way to the Forum, Superman III*, as the Little Man in *Carry On Don't Lose Your Head* and Henry in *Carry On Loving*. Although he concentrated on comedy, he appeared occasionally in TV drama. Died of a heart attack in 1991, aged 72.

ATTENTION!

'Arthur Lowe was a very generous actor. I played Mrs Cole, one of the air raid wardens, in a scene in the church hall office where the telephone kept ringing. I'd never worked with him before, and while rehearsing he must have noticed me frown or something, because he said: "Wait a minute, Rose isn't happy." He asked what the problem was, it was something to do with the timing of me picking up the phone, and ensured I was happy before proceeding. It was nice to see such a fine actor give me, just in a small part, such attention – I was bowled over by him.' **ROSE HILL**

LEON CORTEZ

(b. London)
Role: Milkman (episode 2);
Small Man (episode 24)

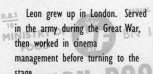

Leon grew up in London. Served in the army during the Great War, then worked in cinema management before turning to the stage.

A well-known Cockney comedian and variety actor, his voice was a familiar one on radio for over three decades with his Cockney Coster Band and his own series *Happy Half-Hour*. Also remembered for his Shakespearean comedy monologues.

On TV, popped up in *Beggar My Neighbour*, *The Saint*, *Dixon of Dock Green* and *The Max Bygraves Show*. He continued to work on the stage throughout his life and toured in the comedy *Doctor at Sea*. Film appearances included *You Can't Help Singing* with Judy Garland.

Leon was due to begin rehearsals for two TV plays when he died in 1970, aged 72.

38. UNINVITED GUESTS

Also appearing: Bill Pertwee (the ARP Warden), Frank Williams (the Vicar), Edward Sinclair (the Verger), Rose Hill (Mrs Cole), Don Estelle (Gerald).

When Hodges' HQ is bombed there is little alternative but to share the church hall with Mainwaring. Unhappy with the situation, Mainwaring complains to the vicar, Area HQ, the Civil Defence people and the secretary of the Council, a fellow Rotarian. The ARP are to leave, but not for a week. Meanwhile Mainwaring and Hodges squabble like kids and the church hall nearly burns down.

39. FALLEN IDOL

Also appearing: Geoffrey Lumsden (Capt. Square), Rex Garner (Capt. Ashley-Jones), Michael Knowles (Capt. Reed), Anthony Sagar (the Sergeant Major), Tom Mennard (the Mess Orderly), Robert Raglan (Capt. Pritchard).

ATTENTION!

'I remember watching *Fallen Idol* being recorded. There is a great scene where a drunk Mainwaring returns to his tent and spins round the tent pole. He didn't have any lines in the script, but during filming spun around the tent pole too much, and said: "Damn these revolving doors." The audience fell about, but the production crew nearly fell off their chairs – he'd put his own line in and it worked beautifully.' **DON ESTELLE**

The platoon attend a weekend course. While the privates consume their free allocation of two pints, Mainwaring is persuaded by Captain Square to distance himself from his men and drink in the officers' mess – much to the disgust of the platoon. In the company of fellow officers, Mainwaring is led astray and ends up drunk. In the morning, nursing a horrific hangover, he's in desperate need of restoring his reputation with his men, something he is able to achieve by saving Jones' life.

CHRISTMAS SPECIAL

Transmitted 27/12/71

40. BATTLE OF THE GIANTS

Also appearing: Bill Pertwee (the ARP Warden), Frank Williams (the Vicar), Edward Sinclair (the Verger), Geoffrey Lumsden (Capt. Square), Robert Raglan (the Colonel), Charles Hill (the Sergeant), Colin Bean (Private Sponge), Rosemary Faith (the Barmaid).

It's the ceremonial church parade and everyone is allowed to wear their medals – the problem is, Mainwaring hasn't got any. After the parade everyone meets up at the pub where Captain Square, Mainwaring's rival at Eastgate, gives Mainwaring stick about his lack of medals and the quality of his platoon. Annoyed by his remarks, Mainwaring agrees to challenge the Eastgate mob in initiation tests, with Hodges, the verger

ARTHUR BROUGH
(b. Petersfield)
Role: Mr Boyle (episode 37)

In his early life, Arthur's great love was acting and running repertory companies. With their wedding money as financial backing, Arthur and his wife opened the East Pavilion, Folkestone, in 1929.

Went on to open successful companies in Leeds, Bradford and Lincoln before the war thwarted any more plans. After demob from the navy, he opened two more reps before branching out into TV and films.

During his career he appeared in several films including *The Green Man* with Alastair Sim, but it's TV for which most people will remember him. Appeared in many bit parts in shows such as *Upstairs, Downstairs* and *The Persuaders*. But for millions of people he'll be remembered as churlish *Mr Grainger* in five years of *Are You Being Served?*

He'd been written in for another series of the sitcom when he died in 1978, six weeks after his wife's death.

and vicar as judges.

Shortly after the tests begin, Jones gets a malaria attack which hampers the platoon's early progress in bursting balloons and filling barrels with feathers. But it's Mainwaring who's first up the tower to raise his flag: trouble is they can't fly it in time. Square beats his adversary and hoists his flag only to find it's got Mainwaring's platoon on it. Walker had supplied the Walmington platoon flag to Square as well!

Arthur Lowe tries to keep young and beautiful.

SEASON FIVE
Transmitted 6/10/72 – 29/12/72

41. ASLEEP IN THE DEEP
Also appearing: Bill Pertwee (the ARP Warden), Colin Bean (Pte. Sponge)

A bomb hits the pumping station where Walker and Godfrey are on patrol. Mainwaring and the rest of the platoon rush to help but the door is blocked. Eventually the rubble is removed and Mainwaring and his men are able to enter the room and free Walker and Godfrey. A further fall of debris traps them all; and when the water pipe bursts and the room rapidly fills with water, time is running out for the intrepid soldiers.

Just as the water nears neck level, Godfrey notices a manhole cover and the platoon flee in the nick of time. But their problems aren't over yet.

42. KEEP YOUNG AND BEAUTIFUL
Also appearing: Bill Pertwee (the ARP Warden), Derek Bond (the Minister), Robert Raglan (the Colonel), James Ottaway (1st MP), Charles Morgan (2nd MP).

Believing the Home Guard is full of old warhorses and the ARP of younger, fitter personnel, Parliament agrees an exchange of men. A parade is planned during which an official from Area HQ will select those to be transferred. With the ageing Walmington-on-Sea platoon likely to be hit hard, everyone makes an effort to look younger. Mainwaring buys a toupee and Wilson wears a corset.

MAINWARING: Wilson, you're wearing corsets, am I right?
WILSON: It's a gentleman's abdominal support.
MAINWARING: Gentleman's abdominal support, my foot, it's corsets. You're a rum cove. You wear that uniform like a sack of porridge and you're as vain as a peacock.
WILSON: It's nothing to do with vanity, sir. I just don't want to be drafted into Hodges' mob, that's all; I'm really rather proud of this platoon. I think you've done wonders getting us all together the way you have – I really mean that. So I just think it pays at the moment not to look any older than one needs.
MAINWARING: I'm sorry, Wilson.
WILSON: That's alright.

MAINWARING: It's very kind of you to pay that tribute to me, very kind. I realise it doesn't come easy to a cold fish like you. And here I am pouring scorn on you. I had no right to really, no right at all. I have to tell you, Wilson, that I too have taken some steps to look a little more . . . a little more virile.
WILSON: Oh my god, it's not monkey glands, is it?
MAINWARING: No! It's nothing as drastic as that. What do you think of this? (*He carefully removes his hat and reveals a ragged wig*)
WILSON: It's awful! (*He begins laughing*) No, no, no, awfully good, it's awfully good (*He subsides into unbridled laughter*)
MAINWARING: Watch it, Wilson, you might snap your girdle!

MARTIN WYLDECK
(b. Birmingham)
Role: Major Regan (episodes 5 & 6)

Martin's father was a Reuters correspondent and the family moved to Innsbruck shortly after he was born. Educated in Austria until the age of 11, Martin returned to England after his father's death to finish his education.

As his first job, he started training as an electrician but decided he wanted to go on the stage, joining Colchester Rep until war broke out. He served in Burma with the army for four years before returning to Colchester.

It didn't take long before he moved into TV. Had his own series with Eleanor Summerfield, *My Wife's Sister*, and appeared in many other shows including *Suez 1956*.

A versatile actor, Martin appeared in over 30 films from 1948 including *Street Corner*, *Carry On Sergeant* (playing Mr Sage, Bob Monkhouse's father) and *Tiffany Jones*.

Martin died in 1988, aged 74. He worked until his death and had just been offered a film role.

ATTENTION!

'I thought Robert was good in the series because the part of the Colonel suited him. The character was like him, a dry sense of humour and a twinkle in the eye. Robert was a very witty, amusing man, and people were always asking him about his time in *Dad's Army*.'
Ms CORNEWALL-WALKER, Robert Raglan's widow

The platoon are worried they'll be transferred, particularly Godfrey, Jones and Frazer, who decide to take drastic action with their appearance.

43. A SOLDIER'S FAREWELL

Also appearing: Bill Pertwee (the ARP Warden), Frank Williams (the Vicar), Robert Gillespie (Charles Boyer), Joan Savage (Greta Garbo), Joy Allen (the Clippie), Colin Bean (Pte. Sponge).

Mainwaring takes the platoon to the cinema but is the only one who remains for the national anthem. Disgusted by their actions, he orders the men to stand to attention during parade while the anthem is played six times.
 After finishing off the night with a cheese supper with Wilson and Jones, Mainwaring goes home to bed. The cheese plays havoc with his stomach and he dreams he's Napoleon.

44. GETTING THE BIRD

Also appearing: Bill Pertwee (the ARP Warden), Frank Williams (the Vicar), Edward Sinclair (the Verger), Pamela Cundell (Mrs Fox), Olive Mercer (Mrs Yeatman), Seretta Wilson (the Wren), Alvar Lidell (the Newsreader).

Wilson is missing and Godfrey reports seeing him with his arm round an attractive blonde. Walker, meanwhile, promises to supply Jones with several dozen pigeons to help his meat supply.
 As Mainwaring tells the men about the voluntary church parade on Sunday, which he expects everyone to attend, a groaning from the stage turns out to be an inebriated Sergeant Wilson.
 Walker and Jones work into the night trying to hide the pigeons away, but Hodges spots the small paraffin light.

HODGES: Oi! Put that ruddy light out, haven't you heard the Jerry planes flying over?
JONES: Well, they can't see a little light like that.

ATTENTION!

'Playing the Clippie was my first TV appearance and I found Clive Dunn very helpful. I was trying to use my theatre voice to project the lines, and he told me quietly to turn my voice right down. Once I did that I was OK.'
JOY ALLEN

In *A Soldier's Farewell* Mainwaring dreamt he was Napoleon.

HODGES: How do you know? Have you been up there to have a look? I'm going to book you for this.

JONES: You're showing more light with that silly torch of yours.

WALKER: *(Passing a couple of pigeons to Hodges)* Come 'ere, have a couple of pigeons and forget it.

HODGES: For me? Oh. Well I suppose . . .

it's not a very big light is it? Ta, thanks very much.

When news reports state a mysterious loss of pigeons from Trafalgar Square, Jones wants nothing more to do with the batch Walker supplied. Finally, the mystery concerning Wilson is cleared up: the mysterious girl is his daughter.

45. THE DESPERATE DRIVE OF CORPORAL JONES

Also appearing: Bill Pertwee (the ARP Warden), Frank Williams (the Vicar), Edward Sinclair (the Verger), Robert Raglan (the Colonel), Larry Martyn (the Signals Private), James Taylor (the Artillery Officer).

The platoon take part in a divisional scheme involving live ammunition. The task is to occupy a deserted barn and defend it against the enemy. But Godfrey and Jones mix up the map references and Mainwaring takes up position in the barn being used as the target for the 25 pounders! Jones and Godfrey, who occupy HQ, desperately try phoning to stop the firing but Godfrey has cut the phone wire by mistake. Jones reaches the barn with just a minute to spare before it's blown to pieces.

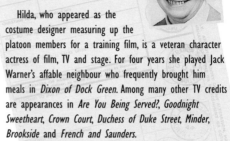

HILDA FENEMORE
(b. London)
Role: Queenie Beal
(episode 67)

Hilda, who appeared as the costume designer measuring up the platoon members for a training film, is a veteran character actress of film, TV and stage. For four years she played Jack Warner's affable neighbour who frequently brought him meals in *Dixon of Dock Green*. Among many other TV credits are appearances in *Are You Being Served?*, *Goodnight Sweetheart*, *Crown Court*, *Duchess of Duke Street*, *Minder*, *Brookside* and *French and Saunders*.

Hilda always wanted to become an actress and when she acted as an amateur in a play directed by Bill Owen (Compo in *Last of the Summer Wine*) everybody thought she was a professional, so she decided to make it her career.

In over four decades in the profession, Hilda — who's still acting — has appeared in 90 films: *Room in the House*, *The Tommy Steele Story*, *Clash by Night* and two *Carry Ons*, Rhoda Bray in *Nurse* and an agitated woman in *Constable*.

ATTENTION!

'People still address me as Mrs Fox. When I was out shopping recently, this man stopped me and asked whether I'd meet his son, a *Dad's Army* fan. This 11-year-old shook my hand and when I asked why he liked the show, he said: "Because it's funny and not rude." That's what makes it so appealing, and we now have a new generation of kids who adore it.'
PAMELA CUNDELL

46. IF THE CAP FITS . . .

Also appearing: Bill Pertwee (the ARP Warden), Campbell Singer (Major General Menzies), Robert Raglan (the Colonel), Edward Sinclair (the Verger), Alex McAvoy (the Sergeant), Dennis Blanch (the 2nd Lieutenant).

Mainwaring is giving a slide show and Frazer isn't happy because it's a lovely summer's evening. After the lecture, he bursts into the office and accuses Mainwaring of wasting time on irrelevant lectures. Mainwaring is furious and fed up with his grousing, so decides to swap rank with Frazer for a few days.

The power soon goes to Frazer's head, as Wilson discovers.

MICHAEL KNOWLES
(b. Midlands)
Role: Capt. Cutts (episodes 9 & 16); Engineer Officer (episode 30); Capt. Reed (episode 39); Capt. Stewart (episode 52)

Michael had considered studying medicine before turning his attention to acting. Graduating from RADA, he worked at reps in Richmond, Bromley and Watford.

Thanks to his time at the Palace Theatre, Watford, Michael was recruited to the cast of *Dad's Army* to play various silly-ass captains. This began a 20-year career in TV, with notable appearances as Capt. Ashwood in *It Ain't Half Hot, Mum,* Fanshaw in BBC's 1978 sitcom, *Come Back, Mrs Noah, The Dick Emery Show* and *Brush Strokes.*

In collaboration with Harold Snoad, he was responsible for adapting 67 episodes for radio. Michael — who's married to Linda James — is still a regular face on TV, particularly in sitcoms.

FRAZER: *(Checking a discrepancy in a record sheet)* You cannot wriggle your way out of this with me. There's a discrepancy: eight yards of four by two missing and unaccounted for.
WILSON: Well I think if you look at the overall . . .
FRAZER: S-t-a-n-d to attention when you're addressing an officer.
WILSON: Well I-I-I might have given a little extra to some of the chaps.
FRAZER: Precisely, incompetence and extravagance – maybe even corruption. Well that's it, you're busted!

The whole platoon get shaken up except for Pikey and Walker who are promoted to rank of corporal and sergeant

respectively. The new Major General, who's taken over area command, arrives at the church hall office and discusses progress with Frazer. He invites him along to the forthcoming Highland get-together and asks him to play the bagpipes.

Eventually Mainwaring slips back into his former role of captain. But what he doesn't realise is that the invitiation to attend the Highland dinner involves playing the bagpipes, which, to Frazer's surprise, he does with consummate ease.

47. THE KING WAS IN HIS COUNTING HOUSE
Also appearing: Bill Pertwee (the ARP Warden), Frank Williams (the Vicar), Edward Sinclair (the Verger), Wendy Richard (Shirley), Colin Bean (Pte. Sponge).

Mainwaring holds a party at his home, a rare occasion. The atmosphere is tense and conversation stilted – perfectly summed up by Walker as resembling 'an undertakers' convention'. But it's brought to an untimely end when the bank takes a direct hit during an air raid. The party guests are recruited to help count the money. With over £96,000 to safeguard, the following day Mainwaring takes it to the Eastgate branch by horse and cart.

48. ALL IS SAFELY GATHERED IN
Also appearing: Bill Pertwee (the ARP Warden), Brenda Cowling (Mrs Prentice), Frank Williams (the Vicar), Edward

Dad's Army

Sinclair (the Verger), Colin Bean (Private Sponge), April Walker (Judy), Tina Cornioli (Olive).

Godfrey requests three days leave to help longtime friend, Mrs Prentice, with her harvest. Realising the importance of the task, Mainwaring gets the whole platoon to help harvest her 100 acres.

Even though Jones falls into the hopper, the gathering of the harvest is a great success. After celebrating with too much potato wine, they join the vicar's service to bless the harvest – but it's rudely interrupted when scuffles breakout in the congregation.

49. WHEN DID YOU LAST SEE YOUR MONEY?

Also appearing: Bill Pertwee (the ARP Warden), Frank Williams (the Vicar), Edward Sinclair (the Verger), Harold Bennett (Mr Blewitt), Tony Hughes (Mr Billings).

The bank is still looking the worse for wear after recently being hit by a bomb, but it's business as usual, even though Mainwaring sits at his desk with an umbrella to protect him from drips.

Jones comes in to deposit £500 collected from local shopkeepers for the town's servicemen's canteen, but the packet he gives Pikey contains sausages but not money – Jones has mislaid the £500.

In an attempt to remember what he's done with the cash, Jones even succumbs to Frazer's suggestion of

The platoon relaxes between scenes.

hypnotism. As a result, it's thought that Mr Blewitt's recently-purchased chicken has been stuffed with the money, but after pulling it apart, that idea falls through. Just as Jones prepares to spend his life's savings on sorting out the problem, the £500 turns up.

ATTENTION!

'I played Mr Billings in *When Did You Last See Your Money?* and remember coming back from lunch during rehearsals to find some of the cast members asleep in their chairs. Someone turned to me and said: "My god, it's like a club for senior citizens, they're all fast asleep!"'

TONY HUGHES

50. BRAIN VERSUS BRAWN

Also appearing: Bill Pertwee (the ARP Warden), Robert Raglan (the Colonel), Edward Sinclair (the Verger), Anthony Roye (Mr Fairbrother), Maggie Don (the Waitress), Geoffrey Hughes (the Bridge Corporal), David Rose (the Dump Corporal).

Wilson is Mainwaring's guest at Walmington's Rotarian dinner at the Peabody Rooms, and Jones and Walker are also there. After getting involved in a discussion with the Colonel regarding not being involved in the new Home Guard commando unit, they accept a challenge to prove that brain is better than brawn. For the exercise, the platoon's objective is to place a bomb in the OC's office. To get past all the guards, they dress up as firemen and travel in a fully-equipped engine. En route, they get diverted by Hodges to a house fire.

51. A BRUSH WITH THE LAW

Also appearing: Bill Pertwee (the ARP Warden), Frank Williams (the Vicar), Edward Sinclair (the Verger), Geoffrey Lumsden (Capt. Square), Jeffrey Gardiner (Mr Wintergreen), Stuart Sherwin (the Junior Warden), Marjorie Wilde (the Lady Magistrate), Chris Gannon (the Clerk of the Court), Toby Perkins (the Usher).

The church hall office light is spotted burning and Hodges takes great pleasure in prosecuting Mainwaring, who decides to defend himself in court. When the verger confesses to Hodges that Mainwaring is innocent, Hodges blackmails him into keeping quiet. Things look grim for Mainwaring until Walker takes the stand as a witness. Having recently supplied whisky to Captain Square, the leading magistrate, Joe's reference to this occasion results in an uneasy Square deciding the case should be dropped. But before matters are wrapped up, the verger confesses to burning the light while compiling his memoirs.

ATTENTION!

'The most difficult day's filming ever was for *Round And Round Went The Great Big Wheel*. We decided that the best way to get the wheel moving was to build a big hub in it and have someone inside peddling. But it didn't work out because the whole mechanism collapsed. From then on we kept pushing and filming it as it gradually slowed down. We could only film about 20 feet of movement at any one time – it took ages!'
DAVID CROFT

52. ROUND AND ROUND WENT THE GREAT BIG WHEEL

Also appearing: Bill Pertwee (the ARP Warden), Geoffrey Chater (Colonel Pierce), Edward Underdown (Major General Sir Charles Holland), Michael Knowles (Capt. Stewart), Jeffrey Segal (the Minister), John Clegg (the Wireless Operator).

The War Office has developed a new weapon: a great explosive-carrying wheel controlled by radio. It can knock out a pillbox within three miles. Operation Catherine Wheel takes place to test the new invention, with Mainwaring's men responsible for fatigues, much to their annoyance.

When Pike and Walker nip off to listen to the radio, they cause interference to the big wheel which rolls out of control, carrying 2000 lbs of high explosives with it. The platoon give chase in their van and that's when the fun begins . . .

53. TIME ON MY HANDS

Also appearing: Bill Pertwee (the ARP Warden), Frank Williams (the Vicar), Edward Sinclair (the Verger), Harold Bennett (Mr Blewitt), Colin Bean (Private Sponge), Joan Cooper (Miss Fortescue), Eric Longworth (Mr Gordon), Christopher Sandford (the German Pilot).

Mainwaring and Wilson's tea break at the Marigold Tea Rooms is interrupted when Pike tells them that a German pilot has bailed out and is hanging from the town hall clock tower. Up in the tower, Mainwaring and his men consider how to pull the pilot to safety. Jones then causes an extra headache by breaking the makeshift ladder, their only route down.

FRAZER: You silly old fool, we'll never get down now. We're marooned, marooned!

JONES: *(Turning to Mainwaring)* Mr Mainwaring, I want to say how sorry I am, and to make up for it I'm going to do anything you tell me to do no matter how dangerous it is. And I'll make any sacrifice in order to regurgitate myself.

They finally retrieve the pilot. Now they have to decide how to get down!

ATTENTION!

'*Time On My Hands* contains quite an elaborate clock with figures moving around every time it strikes. How to make the figures presented us with a problem. We considered plaster, cement and wood before I came up with the idea of employing some midgets. It worked well.' **DAVID CROFT**

Jones was always first to volunteer his services.

ARNOLD RIDLEY

Private Charles Godfrey – a perfect gentleman with over 35 years of service in men's outfitting, courtesy of the Army and Navy Store – possesses a kind, welcoming face. His amiable manner is occasionally derided by the more vociferous members of the platoon, particularly Frazer, who once claimed that he was as 'soft as a cream puff'. When it was discovered he'd been awarded the Military Medal for bravery as a stretcher bearer during the Great War, he was installed as the platoon's medical orderly.

Godfrey lives in a cottage on the outskirts of town with his geriatric sisters, Dolly and Cissy, makers of the famous upside-down cakes. He may be the frailest platoon member, miss parades due to appointments at the clinic, have the weakest bladder (he's always asking to be excused) and too polite to present any kind of threat to the enemy, but his loyalty and dedication are commendable.

When asked whether there were any similarities between Arnold and the excessively delicate Private Godfrey, his widow, Althea, is quick to shake her head. 'He was gentle and kind like Godfrey, but that's where the likeness ends. He was much tougher and not a silly old man at all.

By the time Arnold Ridley joined the ranks of Walmington's Home Guard he was already in his seventies and the oldest member of the cast. Although an established actor and playwright, he was grateful for the chance to appear in BBC's new sitcom, *Dad's Army*.

Arnold, born in Bath in 1896, was educated at Bath and Bristol University, where he began his acting career. For a while after graduating he was uncertain where his future lay: after a short spell teaching, he turned briefly to acting, making his debut in *Prunella* at Bristol's Theatre Royal.

During the First World War he served in the army, but was invalided out in 1917 after being severely wounded at the Somme. 'Sadly, the injuries to his left arm meant it was virtually useless,' recalls Althea Ridley. 'He was also hit in the head by a rifle butt which led to blackouts affecting him for the rest of his life.'

Arnold resumed his acting career in 1918 at Birmingham Rep. During his two years at the company he appeared in over 40 productions. But a year at Plymouth was brought to an abrupt end when forced to give up acting because of his war injuries.

With his life in turmoil, he returned to Bath and worked in his father's boot shop while contemplating a future that looked bleak. But success was soon bestowed upon Arnold. He began writing plays, and although his first attempt was unsuccessful, the second struck gold.

In 1923, Arnold penned *The Ghost Train,* which eventually became a worldwide success and was adapted for both the big and small screen. The idea emerged from an unwelcome wait of several hours at a deserted West Country railway station. Althea recalls: 'He got bored to tears waiting for a train. It was late at night and the atmosphere a little chilling – that experience inspired him to write the play.'

Over the years many productions of *The*

ROBERT RAGLAN (b. Reigate)
Role: H.G. Sgt. (episode 28);
Capt. Pritchard (episodes 37 & 39);
The Colonel (14 episodes)

After joining a water company office straight from school, Robert — whose brother James was also an actor — left to attend drama school. He worked in various reps until war broke out, during which he served in the REME before touring overseas with ENSA.

Frequently cast as policemen or military officials, he resumed his acting career after demob and quickly made his film debut. An illustrious big screen career boasts over 70 films, including *Brothers in Law*, *Private's Progress*, *A Night to Remember* and *Jigsaw*.

After suffering two heart attacks while appearing with Robert Morley in the West End, he retired from the stage and concentrated on TV in shows such as *George and Mildred*, *Shelley* and *Bless this House*.

Although he never starred in any production he was always a solid, dependable supporting actor. He died in 1985.

Ghost Train have been staged, but Arnold's career as a playwright produced more than 30 plays, including *Easy Money* and *Beggar My Neighbour*. 'In time, he became rather bored that all people kept referring to was *The Ghost Train*. He wrote lots of plays but they never seemed to get a mention,' says Althea, who was Arnold's third wife.

In the mid-1930s, he established his own film company with a partner. Their first release, *Royal Eagle,* was favourably received by the critics, but the company's life was brief. During the making of their second film, the bank who had acted as financial backers went bankrupt, leaving Arnold and his partner seriously in debt. It took nearly

Arnold Ridley in comic costume.

THERESE McMURRAY
(b. Herne Bay)

Role: Girl at the Window
(episodes 5 & 6); Girl in the
Haystack (episode 20)

Therese, who made her acting debut in *Snow White* while at St Mary's Convent, Whitstable, believes it was a foregone conclusion that she would become an actress. Previous generations had had successful stage careers including her aunt, who was the world famous contortionist, Cochran's Eve.

She grew up in Whitstable and was attending Saturday drama classes at The Italia Conti Stage School when Lord Grade, her godfather, offered to pay the fees for five years full-time tuition.

She quickly established herself as a leading child actress and appeared in many stage and TV productions. At 18 was cast as Nurse Parkin in *Emergency – Ward 10* where she stayed for two years. In 1968 she kept the nurse's uniform for an appearance in *Hugh and I Spy*, produced by David Croft, which led to the first of her appearances in *Dad's Army*.

Other TV credits include two series of *The Dick Emery Show, Second Time Around, Are You Being Served?* and *The Brighton Belles.*

Married to actor Donald Hewlett, Therese retired from acting in 1981 to bring up her family. She now runs a production company, writing and producing corporate videos.

20 years of Arnold's life to clear the final debt.

When the Second World War began, Arnold was quick to rejoin the army. While serving in France he suffered extreme shell shock and was again discharged.

For the remaining war years Arnold worked with ENSA, and while directing his own play *The Ghost Train,* he met his wife-to-be. 'I went along to the auditions at London's Drury Lane Theatre,' Althea recalls, 'and as I walked up to the door this man opened it for me. Thinking he was the doorman I thanked him and whisked

by. I couldn't believe it when I found out it was Arnold and he was actually directing the play.'

Soon after the war ended, Arnold and Althea wed and he resumed his acting career. Although he'll forever be remembered for *Dad's Army,* the writing of *The Ghost Train* and a career heavily slanted towards the theatre, Arnold also made a handful of films, notably: *Interrupted Journey, The Man Who Knew Too Much* and 1973's *Carry On Girls,* playing the decrepit Alderman Pratt.

On the radio he spent over two decades as Doughy Hood in *The Archers,* and on TV was also seen playing the vicar in *Crossroads* and two characters in *Coronation Street*, Herbert Whittle, who tried courting Minnie Caldwell, in 1967 and John Gilbert in 1969.

Arnold had reached the age of 88 when he died in 1984. Althea has blotted this part of life from her memory. 'We'd been together such a long time that his death was an awful shock. Even now I miss him terribly.'

Ask people who their favourite character is in *Dad's Army*, and a great number will reply 'Godfrey'. Although the character had been sketched out by the time Arnold stepped up to play it, he was responsible for bringing the character alive. With a gentle style of acting and subtle mannerisms, audiences were constantly feeling sorry for poor old Godfrey, particularly when he was often the target for the harsh rebukes dished out by Captain Mainwaring.

Among the viewers he endeared were many children. 'He got lots of fan mail, particularly from children,' Althea says. 'They loved him. He was a fairly private man but never minded children coming up to him in the street. Without a doubt, Arnold loved playing Godfrey.'

CROFT ON RIDLEY

Arnold was a distinguished actor in the theatre, had written successful plays and directed many films. When he came to me he was in his seventies and I explained that I couldn't save him from being required to run about from time to time and did he think he could manage it? 'Oh yes, I think so,' he replied gently, and manage it he did for the next nine years.

Arnold Ridley, as he looked in 1939.

At one stage he had to have an operation and he arrived for filming flat on his back in a large limousine. We propped him up against a tree and photographed him looking left, right, up and down and permanently worried which served as reaction shots to all the situations required for the next week or two. I then sent him home and he returned to us later as game as ever. He had the disconcerting habit of walking up and down impatiently during filming muttering, 'Tell them to get on with it,' which is probably why I got the reputation of being 'One Take Croft'!

IAN LAVENDER

Frank Pike, clerk at the Swallow Bank, is the archetypal mummy's boy. The thumb-sucking, scarf-wearing Pikey is the platoon's youngest member; although he's now in his late teens, he still tends to think of his time with the Walmington-on-Sea Home Guard as an epic adventure straight out of one of his comics. As well as comic reading, Frank's a keen moviegoer who's constantly mollycoddled by his over-protective mother.

Born in Birmingham in 1946, the son of a policeman, Ian thought for a while that he wanted to be a detective. But that idea was soon dropped upon realising he would have to train as a policeman first.

'I've no idea why I wanted to be an actor, but once I'd rid myself of any thoughts of becoming a detective, that was all I thought about,' says Ian.

After finishing his schooling, Ian headed for drama school at Bristol's Old Vic. A season at the Marlowe Theatre, Canterbury followed graduation.

In 1968, his TV debut, a play called *Flowers At My Feet,* was a memorable occasion. Thinking he only had a bit part, Ian was shocked to discover that because an actor had dropped out, he'd

been recast in the leading role. 'I hadn't even read the whole play,' laughs Ian. 'When I turned up for the read-through, I soon realised I had some work to do.

'But the worst thing was that the producer wanted to change my name because he didn't think: "Ian Lavender in *Flowers At My Feet*" sounded right!'

During the same year, Ian was interviewed for the role of Pike in *Dad's Army.* After filming a commercial advertising *Woman's Own* – for which he had to spread marmalade on corn flakes – he phoned his agent to discover he'd got the part of Pike. 'I was excited at the prospect of a whole series on television.'

The existence of a platoon member so young was based on Jimmy Perry's own experience as a teenager in the Home Guard. Ian enjoyed bringing the character to life, though he balked at some of the things he was asked to do. 'For example, I know Jimmy and David wanted Pike to suck his thumb more than I actually did. But despite what the critics said, I never thought of Pike as an idiot; he was more sheltered, naïve; I tried making everything he did logical.'

At the time, Ian didn't think of the role as his big TV break. 'I saw it purely from an economic viewpoint: the offer of several weeks' television work for so much money and the chance that it

might lead to more work. Whereas mates were getting a play or one episode of *Z Cars,* I'd secured several episodes – that's all it meant to me at the time.'

After Ian had researched the Home Guard at London's Imperial War Museum, he duly recorded the first series in 1968. 'The day after transmission I expected to walk around West Kensington and be recognised by everyone, but not a thing!

'As far as fan mail was concerned, nothing happened until about the third or fourth series, by which time the programme had really taken off. I always got letters from young girls or older ladies, never anything in between. Sadly, I was not an idol for nubile 18-year-olds!' laughs Ian.

One of the challenges Ian faced when playing Pike was how to cover his grey hair. 'I turned grey at a very young age so while playing Pike I had to use colour spray and Brylcreem, which works wonders because it shines and reflects the light. But I had to dye it for the stage show and film.'

It was during the fourth season of *Dad's Army* in 1970 that Ian began realising that the

Ian Lavender shows how not to hold a gun.

reaction the show was getting wasn't the norm. 'People wanted to talk about it all the time,' he says. 'I was getting invites to various charity events, along with other comedy actors, but I noticed that people's reaction to me as opposed to them, mainly in the words they used, was different!

'People would approach mates of mine, like Malcolm McFee of *Please, Sir*, and say: "Oh, that was dead funny last week." But to me it would be: "We do love your show." It was an affection that people had for it, rather than simply regarding it as just a funny show.

'I don't think it was ever the funniest thing on TV, but the important factor was that everybody could watch it, and still can,' says Ian. 'It's ideal family viewing.'

To prove the point, Ian recalls a recent visit to a friend's home. 'His children range from age

ALAN TILVERN
(b. London)

Role: Capt. Rodrigues (episode 14); US Colonel (episode 55)

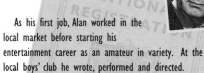

As his first job, Alan worked in the local market before starting his entertainment career as an amateur in variety. At the local boys' club he wrote, performed and directed.

Turning professional in his twenties, his first two assignments were three months at Manchester Rep and a year at Oldham. After various theatre tours he moved into TV and was regularly employed. His aptitude for accents meant he was often cast as foreign characters, particularly Americans and Russians.

His film credits include: *The Black Rose, Superman, Chase a Crooked Shadow, Desert Mice* and *Hot Enough for June*. On TV he's appeared in *Espionage, Maigret* and *No Hiding Place*.

Alan is also a qualified BBC director, and has directed for TV. Recent work has mainly been on the radio.

DAVID DAVENPORT
(b. Berkhamsted)

Role: The Military Police Sgt. (episode 4)

Educated at Berkhamsted School and Stowe College, David was 12 when given ballet lessons by his mother's friend, dancer Anton Dolin. After a year at college, David left to join London's Cone Ripman Ballet School full-time.

By 1938 he was dancing with the Lydia Kyasht Russian Ballet, and four years later the Royal Ballet. During a glittering dancing career he appeared with Margot Fonteyn and Robert Helpmann in various performances including *Miracle in the Gorbals*.

Four years (1942–46) as a wireless operator in the RAF, interrupted his dancing career, which he then resumed until concentrating on the musical stage in the early 1950s. Soon his talent had spread to films and TV.

Film credits include: *Carry On Cleo* (as Bilius), *Carry On Henry* (as Major Domo), *King's Rhapsody* and *You Only Live Twice*. On TV he's perhaps best remembered as Malcolm Ryder, Noele Gordon's husband, in *Crossroads*. But he appeared in many other shows, including *All Creatures Great and Small*.

David's final West End appearance was in *The Secret Diary of Adrian Mole* in 1986. Bad health prevented him ever working again.

four to eight, and they know the episodes and even the film off by heart. They quote lines at me, and when they put a video on it's always an episode of the show.'

One of the sitcom's greatest strengths, in Ian's eyes, is the pairing of Mainwaring and Wilson. 'They worked so well together, and their own relationship complemented the partnership. Arthur and John weren't bosom buddies or natural social companions, but they liked each other and worked extremely well together. In the show they weren't the best of friends but they had been flung together and couldn't escape – it was inspired casting and writing.'

Ian was terrified when filming began because here he was, a callow actor, not long out of drama school, working with the likes of John Le Mesurier, John Laurie and Arthur Lowe. But he needn't have worried. 'Everyone took me under their wings right from the start and looked after me, they were wonderful.

'Arthur gave me my greatest piece of advice. During the first series I had little to do,' explains Ian. 'One day he came over and said: "Look, don't worry if you haven't got much to do at the moment, that will come. Meanwhile get yourself a funny costume and stand near me."

'So when asked to go and choose a scarf from the wardrobe department, I picked one with loud, clashing colours. I also ordered this awful garish orange cricketing jumper. I'm colourblind but I knew the colours clashed terribly.' Ian feels that following Arthur's advice helped in the character's overall development.

Someone who joined the cast in 1972 and was looking forward to finding out what the actor behind Pikey was really like was Eric Longworth, who played the Town Clerk. 'Before I joined the cast I watched Dad's Army regularly and the person I most wanted to meet was Ian. I was interested to find out what he was like in real life. He was so opposite to Pikey, a marvellous characterisation that he'd created all on his own.'

Since hanging up his scarf, Ian has been heard on the radio and seen in various small screen comedies, including two episodes of Yes, Minister. A sizeable chunk of his time and earnings is concerned with directing and acting in pantomimes. But because he hasn't been seen in any recent long-running TV role, many people think that playing Pike for so long has held back his career.

'Twenty years since it finished, I am still making quite a good living and not exactly scraping about for work. Essentially I'm offered comedy because that's what people know me for; I don't get many chances to play Hamlet, so, yes, I've been held back in some ways. But what about all the work I've done because of playing Pike.'

So Ian will always be grateful to Dad's Army. 'I was particularly pleased that success happened for me early, for my father's sake. He'd been through two World Wars, a Depression and had been against me attending drama school, so I was a success in his eyes before he died and for that I'm grateful.'

CROFT ON LAVENDER

Ian was a client of Ann, my wife, who was an agent at that time. When Dad's Army was scheduled for production she insisted that I watch a TV drama in which Ian gave a sensitive and charming performance. She sent him to me and I thought him just right to play Pike and he got the part. Being much younger than the rest of the cast, he was not a little daunted by their vast experience. He realised that he would disappear as an artist unless he quickly found a character for Pike and fought for his survival. Accordingly he appeared on the first day of filming with the now famous scarf and with his cap firmly on the centre of his head looking like a complete nerd. Lovely touches like sucking his thumb when asleep quickly followed until he'd built up a completely believable and true portrait of a late teenager earnestly playing at being a soldier. He was always a great pleasure to direct and write for.

A scene from the episode
Knights Of Madness.

Series Guide: SEASONS 6-9

SEASON SIX

Transmitted 31/10/73 – 12/12/73

54. THE DEADLY ATTACHMENT

Featuring: Philip Madoc (U-boat Captain). Also appearing: Bill Pertwee (Chief Warden Hodges), Edward Sinclair (the Verger), Robert Raglan (the Colonel), Colin Bean (Pte Sponge).

Mainwaring is responsible for guarding a brusque U-boat captain and seven crew, who've been drifting in a dinghy for two days, until an armed escort arrives. When the escort is delayed until the next morning, the platoon has to guard them all night – Mainwaring exchanges a few words with the captain.

U-BOAT CAPTAIN: I am making notes, Captain, and your name will go on the list; and when we win the war you'll be brought to account.
MAINWARING: You can write what you like, you're not going to win the war.
U-BOAT CAPTAIN: Oh yes we are.
MAINWARING: Oh no you're not.
U-BOAT CAPTAIN: Oh yes we are!
PIKE: (Singing) Whistle while you work,

Hitler is a twerp, he's half barmy, so is his army, whistle while you work.
U-BOAT CAPTAIN: You're name will also go on the list, what is it?
MAINWARING: Don't tell him, Pike.
U-BOAT CAPTAIN: Pike! (He writes it down).

Walker heads off to the chippie to buy fish and chips for everyone before settling down for the long night. Later, when the U-boat Captain collapses on the floor complaining of stomach pains, Mainwaring has to decide whether this is just another Nazi trick.

ATTENTION!

'I have two favourite episodes, and *The Deadly Attachment* is one. The line where Mainwaring says: "Don't tell him, Pike!" has been a constant source of amusement. Even now, people shout it at me across the street, and I didn't even say it! Just one line in one episode, and people remember it. We all loved the filming, particularly the idea of ordering fish and chips. During one scene I began to laugh; I begged David Croft to edit the bit out but he didn't.'
IAN LAVENDER

55. MY BRITISH BUDDY

Also appearing: Bill Pertwee (Chief Warden Hodges), Alan Tilvern (US Colonel), Frank Williams (the Vicar), Edward Sinclair (the Verger), Janet Davies (Mrs Pike), Wendy Richard (Shirley), Pamela Cundell (Mrs Fox), Verne Morgan (the Landlord), Talfryn Thomas (Mr Cheeseman), Suzanne Kerchiss (Ivy), Robert Raglan (the Colonel), Blain Fairman (the US Sergeant).

The Americans have joined the fight against the Germans and a darts match is arranged at the Red Lion to welcome a small advance party. After the formal introductions, Mainwaring tells the Americans to make themselves at home, so they rush over to the girls – who happen to be the platoon members' partners. When the American colonel complains about the warm beer and Hodges mouths off about the slowness of the Yanks in joining the war, a fight breaks out. Thanks to Mr Cheeseman of the *Eastbourne Gazette*, who was attending the party, extensive coverage of the incident appears in the local rag.

ATTENTION!

When the series began in 1968, Jimmy Perry and David Croft were paid £400 per script.

GEOFFREY LUMSDEN
(b. London)
Role: Colonel Square (episode 3); Corporal-Colonel Square (episodes 11 & 12); Captain Square (episodes 28, 39, 40, 51, 75)

Geoffrey's character was a guffawing old war veteran who had taken charge of the Home Guard's Eastgate platoon. There was intense rivalry and constant tension between Square and Mainwaring, partly because Square always pronounced his rival's name wrong.

By the time Geoffrey left school both his parents had died, so he stayed with his uncle. Against his wishes he worked at a colliery training as an engineer. Whilst there, he helped organise several concerts. Realising his future lay in the entertainment world, he left the mines and won a scholarship to RADA.

His busy rep career was interrupted when the war began. But after serving with the army in Burma he returned to rep at Dundee.

Geoffrey, who was also a playwright, moved into TV and most notably worked in *Sykes* and *Edward and Mrs Simpson*. He also appeared with Ray Milland in the 1968 movie *Hostile Witness*. He died in 1984.

56. THE ROYAL TRAIN

Also appearing: Bill Pertwee (Chief Warden Hodges), Frank Williams (the Vicar), Edward Sinclair (the Verger), William Moore (the Station Master), Freddie Earlle (Henry), Ronnie Brody (Bob), Fred McNaughton (the Mayor), Sue Bishop (the Ticket Collector), Bob Hornery (the City Gent).

With King George VI passing through Walmington-on-Sea on the Royal Train, Mainwaring's men provide the Guard of Honour. When a train's whistle is heard in the distance they line up before realising it's a false alarm. The engine stops and the drivers go to the office to make a phone call and have a quick

ATTENTION!

'This is one of my favourite episodes, partly because of the location filming. It was quite alarming going up and down the railway line on the pump truck. Part of the scene shows the train in reverse chasing the truck, which I was on with some others. I remember Bill Pertwee saying: "It's gaining on us, it's gaining on us, it's going to run in to us if we're not careful." Of course, we were in no danger but for a while it seemed like it!' **FRANK WILLIAMS**

The platoon compete in an efficiency test and take their Smith gun along. When Mainwaring opens the door of Jones' van, hundreds of onions, Walker's order for Hodges, fall out. If the men pass the test with flying colours, they'll be graded a 12-star platoon. After early set backs while negotiating an electric fence and attacking the NAAFI teagirl, who they suspect of carrying a bomb in disguise, they pick up marks for showing initiative when firing Walker's onions at an advancing line of troops. But is it enough to earn them their 12-star goal?

cuppa. Mistaking Mainwaring's sleeping pills for saccharin they're quickly asleep in their chairs leaving no alternative but for the Home Guard to move their train in order to clear the line for the King.

Pike is the only one who can drive the engine, the trouble is he can't stop it. After some hair-raising moments, they manage to stop just in time to see the King go racing by.

57. WE KNOW OUR ONIONS

Also appearing: Fulton Mackay (Capt. Ramsey), Bill Pertwee (Chief Warden Hodges), Edward Sinclair (the Verger), Alex McAvoy (the Sergeant), Pamela Manson (the NAAFI Girl), Cy Town (the Mess Steward).

ATTENTION!

When the first series was screened, John Le Mesurier was earning more than Arthur Lowe. They received £262.10 and £210 respectively. Eventually Lowe was the highest paid cast member.

As Captain Ramsey, Fulton Mackay inspects the platoon's onion-firing capability.

58. THE HONOURABLE MAN

Also appearing: Bill Pertwee (Chief Warden Hodges), Frank Williams (the Vicar) Edward Sinclair (the Verger), Eric Longworth (the Town Clerk), Janet Davies (Mrs Pike), Gabor Vernon (the Russian), Hana-Maria Pravda (the Interpreter), Robert Raglan (the Colonel), Pamela Cundell (Mrs Fox), Fred McNaughton (the Mayor).

Mainwaring heads a committee set up to greet a celebrated Russian visiting Walmington. Frazer suggests giving him a £10 voucher towards funeral expenses,

Mrs Fox, representing the WVS, feels everyone should smile a lot, while Godfrey's not sympathetic to the Reds. Mainwaring takes the suggestions away to consider the best plan. At the bank a letter arrives addressed to The Honourable Arthur Wilson, the result of an uncle dying which has moved his family up the social ladder. Mainwaring can't believe it.

WILSON: I don't really see why it should make any difference to you and me.
MAINWARING: You can bet your bottom dollar it won't make any difference to you and me. (Getting agitated) And you needn't think you can roll in here 20

ATTENTION!

'The real chink in Mainwaring's armour is he cannot handle the fact that Wilson is a public schoolboy – it's his real hang-up. This episode makes the most of that: we really see Mainwaring the fighter, the British bulldog, because he's cut to the quick by this business of Wilson getting a title. Mainwaring goes for Wilson's jugular and this episode typifies the relationship between Mainwaring and Wilson, a major part of what *Dad's Army* is about.' **STEPHEN LOWE**

DON ESTELLE (b. Manchester)
Role: The Man from Pickfords (episode 19); 2nd ARP Warden (episode 28); Gerald (episodes 36 & 38)

Don, who sang from childhood, worked as an amateur singer at night in clubs during the 1950s, while working for a soft furnishing company during the day.

After writing to Granada TV, he was given work as an extra in *Coronation Street* and television plays. But Don will always be grateful to Arthur Lowe for helping lift his career from being a stand-up singer working the club circuit and occasional extra, to speaking parts on TV.

While appearing as an extra in *Coronation Street*, Don, on Arthur's advice, wrote to David Croft enquiring about a part in *Dad's Army* – shortly after he got a job.

Initially appearing as a removal man delivering a naval gun, he returned three times, establishing a semi-character called Gerald, who reported to Hodges.

But Don's best known for playing Lofty in *It Ain't Half Hot, Mum*, and the subsequent spin-off record with Windsor Davies, *Whispering Grass*, which topped the charts in 1975.

Nowadays, he still sings around the world and runs his own music publishing company.

minutes late after lunch. Where have you been?
WILSON: Well, I went up to the golf club and had a bite to eat up there.
MAINWARING: The golf club!
WILSON: Yes.
MAINWARING: Who took you?
WILSON: Well I'm a member.
MAINWARING: You're a member, since when?
WILSON: Yes, well you see, when the committee heard about this title thing, they asked me if, you know, I'd like to join.
MAINWARING: (Red in fury) I've been trying for years to get in there.
WILSON: I believe they're awfully particular!

It seems everyone thinks the newy-titled Wilson should present the key allowing the visitor the freedom of the town and, although Mainwaring fights against it, Wilson comes out on top again.

59. THINGS THAT GO BUMP IN THE NIGHT

Also appearing: Jonathan Cecil (Captain Cadbury), Colin Bean (Pte Sponge).

It's a stormy night for driving and with petrol running out the platoon take shelter in an old house.

MAINWARING: Sponge!
SPONGE: Yes, Captain Mainwaring.
MAINWARING: Didn't you fill the tank yesterday?
SPONGE: I didn't have any coupons.
MAINWARING: But Walker was supposed to be supplying the coupons.
PIKE: Ah, yeah . . . he couldn't get the ink dry in time!

As a pack of dogs howls outside, the house appears empty except for the burning fire.

ATTENTION!

'*Dad's Army* is one of the favourite things I've done. I'd been doing a lot of theatre and working during the evenings in those pre-video days meant I hadn't seen the show much. When I was asked to play the part I felt uncertain because the guest roles tended to be rather small. So I phoned my late father, who was a great fan, and he said: "Whatever the part, do it." It turned out to be a great role. I think the bloodhounds had been fed before filming because they found it difficult to run – and when they did it was often in the wrong direction!' **JONATHAN CECIL**

STUART SHERWIN
(b. Stoke-on-Trent)

Role: 2nd ARP Warden (episodes 22, 23 & 33); Junior Warden (episode 51)

Stuart's father was a pottery salesman travelling the country. When he arrived home on Fridays, the family would visit the local theatre, and that's where Stuart's interest in the stage originated.

Before joining the army during the Second World War, he worked on the railways in various jobs including a booking clerk. Returned to the job for a while after demob until moving to an estate agents. Eventually he joined a rep company in Leeds after applying to an advert in *The Stage*.

His final spell in rep was a winter season at Bognor after which he toured in *Salad Days* in 1960. Small parts in TV came along including a role in *Emergency — Ward 10*.

Since *Dad's Army* he's worked for Les Dawson, Terry Scott, appeared in *Keeping Up Appearances*, as a clerk of the court in *Rumpole of the Bailey* and as a hotel guest in *Fawlty Towers*.

Although he recently filmed a part in *The Find*, the last few years have been dominated by long stints in theatre. He's just finished a two-year spell in *Oliver!* at the Palladium.

When someone enters the house and climbs the stairs, the platoon wait nervously – but it turns out to be Captain Cadbury. In the morning, he tells them it's a school for training tracker dogs. As the platoon go off to collect some petrol the dogs get loose and give chase – the problem is they aren't fully trained and are still inclined to tear their victims apart!

60. THE RECRUIT

Also appearing: Bill Pertwee (Chief Warden Hodges), Frank Williams (the Vicar), Edward Sinclair (the Verger), Susan Majolier (the Nurse), Lindsey Dunn (the small boy).

Mainwaring is in hospital with ingrowing toenails and his trusty old pistol by his

The vicar and the verger.

The verger joins the platoon at the bar.

side. Wilson is in charge of the platoon, who aren't happy when he allows the vicar and verger to join the ranks. They arrive for their first parade.

VICAR: *(He runs into the office)* Oh dear, I'm so sorry I'm late, the confirmation class went on and on and on – have I missed anything?
WILSON: It's perfectly all right, we're just going to start the parade now.
VICAR: Oh, how very exciting.
VERGER: *(Comes rushing in)* You left your belt in the vestry, your reverence.
VICAR: Oh, silly me.
WILSON: All right, now that you're both here we can start.
VICAR: Goody, goody.

Mainwaring arrives at the hall, he's discharged himself early. Unhappy with the new additions, he aims to remove them. That evening they're on patrol with Jones' section. While the verger and vicar are on guard an impudent kid gives them lip. The verger clips him round the ear and he rushes off to tell his Uncle Willie – who turns out to be Hodges. Mainwaring feels the Vicar should have dealt with the matter better – taking offence, the new recruits resign.

ATTENTION!

For the first series, Clive Dunn was paid £210 per episode, John Laurie £105, Jimmy Beck £78 and Arnold Ridley £63.

SEASON SEVEN

Transmitted 15/11/74 – 23/12/74

61. EVERYBODY'S TRUCKING

Also appearing: Bill Pertwee (Chief Warden Hodges), Frank Williams (the Vicar), Edward Sinclair (the Verger), Pamela Cundell (Mrs Fox), Harold Bennett (Mr Bluett), Olive Mercer (Mrs Yeatman), Felix Bowness (the Driver), Colin Bean (Private Sponge).

Mainwaring's men are asked to signpost the route for an exercise the regulars are having in the area. After completing the job they discover the route is blocked by an unmanned steam engine, the driver having left it to get some coal. In an

ATTENTION!

'The first time I was on location I laughed during the recording of a scene. It was such a funny scene, but it wasn't the thing to do and it had to be shot again. I thought I'd better move away and decided to climb a nearby tree. I'm a good bird whistler so started whistling away until Bill Pertwee came over and told me to stop because it would be heard on the film. When the location shots were shown during the studio recording, you could hear a bird – that was me!'
FELIX BOWNESS

FELIX BOWNESS (b. Harwell)
Role: Driver (episode 61); Special Constable (episode 67); Van Driver (episode 79)

Felix has been in the entertainment business for over four decades, performing in variety shows around the country. A veteran warm-up man, winning a talent contest in Reading led to him turning semi-pro. Whilst working in cabaret, he was spotted by a BBC producer and given a small part in radio.

With great tenacity, Felix — an amateur boxing champion in his late teens — kept plugging away, eventually making his TV debut as a stand-up comic before moving into comedy roles in shows like *Porridge*, playing Gay Gordon.

Felix, best known as jockey Fred Quilley in *Hi-De-Hi!*, has worked often for Perry and/or Croft: he was a customer in *Are You Being Served?*, a grocer in *You Rang, M'Lord?* and also in *Hugh and I*.

A relief guard in the last series of *Oh, Doctor Beeching!*, Felix will be warming up the audiences for the new series.

attempt to drive round the engine Jones' van gets stuck in the mud; and before long so has Hodges' van, his motorbike and sidecar as well as a coach carrying a group of pensioners on their annual trip. After many failed attempts to sort the trouble out, there's no alternative but to set up a diversion.

62. A MAN OF ACTION

Also appearing: Bill Pertwee (Chief Warden Hodges), Talfryn Thomas (Mr Cheeseman), Frank Williams (the Vicar), Edward Sinclair (the Verger), Eric Longworth (the Town Clerk), Harold Bennett (Mr Bluett), Arnold Peters (Fire Officer Dale), Jay Denyer (Inspector Baker), Robert Mill (Capt. Swan), Colin Bean (Private Sponge).

Pike, on patrol with Jones, relives a childhood memory by pushing his head through an ironbar gate – only this time he gets stuck! Mainwaring and Wilson discuss the arrival of a temporary recruit, Mr Cheeseman, from the *Eastbourne Gazette*. He's doing a weekly article about the platoon. As Mainwaring prepares to have his photo taken, Jones telephones and he rushes off to help. To keep the embarrassing incident to themselves, they take the gate from its hinges and march back to the church hall. While Pike sits and waits for someone to free him, Mainwaring rushes in to an emergency meeting being held in the church hall office: a land mine has ripped up 100 yards of railway track; gas and water supplies have been cut off and the phone wires are down. As the town is cut off, Mainwaring declares martial law.

ATTENTION!

'The production was well organised. All the characters were beautifully related to each other and the merest look or word would be a cue for a laugh. But I remember David Croft was anxious that scenes which wouldn't create a laugh, namely me marching or whatever, should be done as expeditiously as possible so it wouldn't encroach on the laughter time!' **ROBERT MILL**

63. GORILLA WARFARE

Also appearing: Bill Pertwee (Chief Warden Hodges), Talfryn Thomas (Private Cheeseman), Edward Sinclair (the Verger), Robert Raglan (the Colonel), Robin Parkinson (Lieutenant Wood), Erik Chitty (Mr Clerk), Rachel Thomas (the Mother Superior), Michael Sharvell-Martin (the Lieutenant), Verne Morgan (the Farmer), Joy Allen (the Lady with the Pram).

The platoon arrive ready for the weekend's exercise. Wilson has brought his pyjamas and eau de Cologne while Godfrey has his eiderdown.

GODFREY: Good afternoon, Captain Mainwaring.
MAINWARING: What are you carrying that eiderdown for?
GODFREY: Well we shall be out all night and my sister Dolly thought it might help keep me warm.
MAINWARING: You can't move swiftly across country loaded down with that.
FRAZER: He couldn't move swiftly across country stark naked!

For the exercise the platoon are commandos behind enemy lines trying to rendezvous with a highly important secret agent, to be played by Mainwaring, who they will escort to a secret destination. GHQ will have counteragents out trying to capture Mainwaring.

Knowing the counteragents are disguised they ignore everyone, including two stranded nuns and a doctor who suddenly appears warning Mainwaring about an escaped gorilla roaming the woods.

The platoon settle down for the night in a barn and Lieutenant Wood, who is dressed up as the gorilla, is confident he'll ruin Mainwaring's plans. After a tangle with the gorilla the following day, Mainwaring leads his men to victory.

ATTENTION!

For her guest appearance in episode six, *Shooting Pains*, Barbara Windsor received £172. Freddie Trueman, meanwhile, was paid £277 for episode 36, *The Test*.

PHILIP MADOC
(b. Merthyr Tydfil)
Role: U-boat Captain (episode 54)

For someone who only appeared in one episode, it's unbelievable how many people recall vividly Philip's role as the U-boat captain.

After working as an interpreter in Germany, he entered the industry in the 1960s, studying at RADA. Worked for a while in rep before moving into TV: one of his first TV appearances was in the 1956 production *The Count of Monte Cristo*. Other TV work includes: Detective Chief Supt. Tate in *Target*, Fison in *A Very British Coup*, *The Avengers* and *Dr Who*.

Also made over 30 films including: *The Quiller Memorandum*, *Daleks: Invasion Earth* and *Operation Daybreak*. Recent years have been dominated by theatre. His own TV detective series, *A Mind to Kill*, in which he plays the lead, has been sold all over the world.

Dad's Army

64. THE GODIVA AFFAIR

Also appearing: Bill Pertwee (Chief Warden Hodges), Talfryn Thomas (Private Cheeseman), Frank Williams (the Vicar), Edward Sinclair (the Verger), Janet Davies (Mrs Pike), Pamela Cundell (Mrs Fox), Eric Longworth (the Town Clerk), Peter Honri (Private Day), Rosemary Faith (the Waitress), Colin Bean (Private Sponge), George Hancock (Private Hancock).

The town is £2000 short of their target for buying a Spitfire so a procession is

Arthur Lowe in a scene with Pamela Cundell (Mrs Fox).

planned with the platoon as morris dancers. After rehearsals, Jones pours out his heart to Mainwaring and Wilson: he suspects widow Mrs Fox, who he'd been 'walking out with' of being smitten with Mr Gordon, the town clerk.

WILSON: What! Not that silly bald-headed old duffer, do you mean?
(Mainwaring removes his hat revealing his shining bald head)
WILSON: *(Staring at Mainwaring's head)* Oh, I don't mean he's a bald-headed old duffer because he's got a bald head . . . I mean he'd be a silly old . . . wouldn't he? . . . I mean . . . he'd be a silly old duffer even if he'd got a full head of hair.
MAINWARING: All right, all right, all right, all right.

Jones begs Mainwaring to speak to Mrs Fox on his behalf; he reluctantly agrees and meets her at the Marigold Tea Rooms the following day. As he stumbles his way through his words, Mrs Fox gets the wrong end of the stick and thinks Mainwaring fancies her.

In the church hall Hodges and his panel of judges are selecting who'll play Lady Godiva in the procession. After a whisper in his ear, the Town Clerk selects the robust Mrs Fox. When on procession day, Mrs Fox finds her fleshings and wig stolen it's Jones she turns to for comfort. But to Mainwaring's consternation, it's his wife who has donned the wig and rides as Lady Godiva!

ATTENTION!

'The Town Clerk was a rather pompous, northerner, but he was wonderful to play. *The Godiva Affair* is my favourite episode. Mrs Fox is auditioning for the part of Lady Godiva. I claim she'll be perfectly respectable covered from top to toe in fleshings and wearing a wig of long golden tresses. I mouthed every syllable of it while drooling over the thought of Mrs Fox with her ample figure wearing fleshings.'
ERIC LONGWORTH

65. THE CAPTAIN'S CAR

Also appearing: Bill Pertwee (Chief Warden Hodges), Talfryn Thomas (Private Cheeseman), Frank Williams (the Vicar), Edward Sinclair (the Verger), Robert Raglan (the Colonel), Eric Longworth (the Town Clerk), Fred McNaughton (the Mayor), Mavis Pugh (Lady Maltby), John Hart Dyke (the French General), Donald Morley (Glossip).

A French general is visiting the town and Mainwaring's platoon is selected to provide a guard of honour, partly because of their smartness and also as a result of Wilson's ability to speak French. Lady Maltby, meanwhile, donates her Rolls to the war effort. Mainwaring decides he'll second it as his staff car. On the day of

JOHN CATER (b. London)
Role: Private Clarke (episode 34)

Private Clarke was an unwelcome visitor to Walmington-on-Sea, casting inaccurate slurs on Jones' military past.

Trained at RADA, John joined Dundee Rep shortly after graduation. His first speaking role on TV was during the 1950s BBC series *The Appleyards*.

John's had a busy career on TV, including the part of batman Doublett in ATV's *Virgin of the Secret Service* in 1968, Starr in *The Duchess of Duke Street*, George Watts in *The Other 'Arf*, *Up Pompeii!*, *Bergerac* and *Shelley*. Has also appeared in over 30 films, including *The Black Tulip* and *The Mill on the Floss*.

Recent TV credits include *Silent Witness* and *Where the Heart Is*. Also seen as Einstein in a recent commercial.

its delivery, the car breaks down and Pike and Wilson rush off to help, ensuring it gets to the paint shop first for camouflaging. Confusion arises when Jones also helps, but tows away the mayor's Rolls instead and gets Frazer to paint it by mistake. When the error is spotted, Frazer repaints it black, but not with quick-drying paint, as the handprints on Hodges' face reveal after he's greeted by the French general.

ATTENTION!

'Jimmy Perry and David Croft were very loyal to people who had worked for them. The part of Lady Maltby, which was actually my first TV role, was designed by Jimmy with me in mind. I'd worked with him at Watford Rep. It was a lovely part.'
MAVIS PUGH

66. TURKEY DINNER

Also appearing: Bill Pertwee (Chief Warden Hodges), Talfryn Thomas (Private Cheeseman), Frank Williams (the Vicar), Edward Sinclair (the Verger), Harold Bennett (Mr Bluett), Pamela Cundell (Mrs Fox), Janet Davies (Mrs Pike), Olive Mercer (Mrs Yeatman), Dave Butler (the Farmhand).

It's confession time: members of the platoon tell Mainwaring about their monumental binge during which they accidentally killed a turkey. Believing the bird could only have belonged to the North Berrington turkey farm, the platoon march to the farm to apologise and pay for the bird. After discovering it didn't belong to the farm, Mainwaring and Wilson discuss what to do with the turkey.

WILSON: Well, Jonesey shot it, I suppose it rightfully belongs to him.
MAINWARING: No, no, he was on duty, he was wearing one of my uniforms, carrying one of my rifles and he fired one of my bullets.
WILSON: I see. Does that mean you're bagging it, sir?
MAINWARING: No, it doesn't mean I'm bagging it – not all of it anyway.
WILSON: In that case, I bags it.
MAINWARING: I'm afraid you can't do that, you see I bags it first.
WILSON: Well you said you didn't want it, anyway you didn't use the word bag, so it doesn't count.
MAINWARING: Now don't start using any of that public school cheating with me.

Mainwaring dishes out the turkey.

The platoon decide to throw a turkey dinner for the OAPs. Although he helps serve, Mainwaring is dressed in a dinner suit ready for a swift exit to a later engagement. But, as expected, things go wrong when Pike throws gravy over Mainwaring and Jones tries to cover the stains with white paint!

ATTENTION!

In the fifth episode, *The Showing Up Of Corporal Jones*, Caroline Dowdeswell appeared in a scene that was cut before transmission. This was the only episode she wasn't seen in during the first season.

SEASON EIGHT

Transmitted 5/9/75 – 10/10/75

67. RING DEM BELLS

Also appearing: Bill Pertwee (Chief Warden Hodges), Frank Williams (the Vicar), Edward Sinclair (the Verger), Jack Haig (the Landlord), Robert Raglan (the Colonel), Felix Bowness (the Special Constable), John Bardon (Harold Forster), Hilda Fenemore (Queenie Beal), Janet Mahoney (the Barmaid), Adele Strong (the Lady with umbrella).

The platoon take part in a training film, playing Nazis, much to Mainwaring's disgust. There's only two officers' uniforms and as they fit Wilson and Pike, they're chosen for the parts. After being told filming has been postponed for a week, the platoon return from location, stopping off at a country pub on the way. The barman at the Six Bells pub understandably mistakes them for real enemy and gets the barmaid to fetch the police.

Mainwaring lays down the law.

'*Ring Dem Bells* is my other favourite episode, purely for practical reasons. Wilson and Pike were chosen to play German officers in a training film because the uniforms fitted. So for five days filming in Norfolk and throughout the studio work, we had comfortable costumes to wear. It was a fun episode.' **IAN LAVENDER**

Mainwaring and his men get away in time, but when Hodges, the vicar and verger spot him talking to a bunch of supposed Germans, they think he's a quisling and sound the church bells.

68. WHEN YOU'VE GOT TO GO

Also appearing: Bill Pertwee (Chief Warden Hodges), Frank Williams (the Vicar), Edward Sinclair (the Verger), Janet Davies (Mrs Pike), Eric Longworth (the Town Clerk), Freddie Earlle (the Italian Sergeant), Tim Barrett (the Doctor), Colin Bean (Private Sponge), Frankie Holmes (the Fishfryer).

Pike gets his call-up papers and has to attend a medical, but Mrs Pike thinks it's just a formality before he's rejected because of his weak ankles and chest, not to mention the nervous twitch he's recently adopted. So she's shocked when

he's passed A1. To celebrate the boy's departure, the platoon hold a fish and chip supper at the local chippie.

But before that the town clerk organises a blood donor session and the rivalry between Hodges and Mainwaring leads to a contest to see who can get the most people to be donors. Just when it looks like Hodges will win, Jones and Frazer come to their captain's rescue by gathering together 17 nuns and a myriad of Italian POWs.

At the chip shop the platoon enjoy their fish and chips until Pikey announces that his recent donation of blood has indicated that he belongs to a rare blood group; he can't join up.

ATTENTION!

'Playing Italians is one of my specialities so I enjoyed this one. But I have vivid memories of the first episode I worked on. I turned up for rehearsals and sat down. When John Laurie arrived I said: "Morning, Mr Laurie." He walked past mumbling. Next morning, the same thing. So I asked Clive Dunn, an old friend, what was wrong. Clive said: "The problem is you're sitting in his chair, he likes sitting there in the corner doing the crossword." I went up to John and apologised. He turned to me and asked where I was from. After replying "Glasgow", he said: "Oh, a fellow Scotsman, you can sit there if you want."' **FREDDIE EARLLE**

Frazer championed Godfrey's cause in episode 69.

69. IS THERE HONEY STILL FOR TEA?

Also appearing: Bill Pertwee (Chief Warden Hodges), Gordon Peters (the man with the door), Robert Raglan (the Colonel), Campbell Singer (Sir Charles McAllister), Joan Cooper (Dolly), Kathleen Sainsbury (Cissy).

Mainwaring is told Godfrey's cottage is to be flattened to make way for a new aerodrome. Intending to break the news, Mainwaring, Wilson and Pike visit Godfrey and his two aged sisters.

After devouring upside down cakes, they leave without broaching the subject, concerned that the gravity of the situation may cause him to keel over. Jones is the one who finally tells Godfrey, by which time he's already received official notice.

JOY ALLEN (b. Werrington)
Role: The Clippie (episode 43); Lady with the Pram (episode 63)}

Joy always wanted to become an actress and upon leaving school took elocution lessons before joining RADA.

After drama school she was offered the chance to join a production of *King's Rhapsody* in two capacities: as an understudy and member of the chorus. Then when the principal girl in a Peterborough panto was taken ill, Joy took over within three days.

Shortly after, Joy got married, raised a family and left the acting profession until the early 1970s when a manager/director of a theatrical company in Corby, Northants, spotted her in an amateur production and invited her to join his company. She stayed three years, by which time she'd made the first of two appearances in *Dad's Army*.

Seen in other TV shows including *Are You Being Served?* and several non-speaking roles. Nowadays works mostly as an extra.

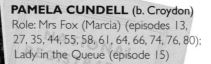

PAMELA CUNDELL (b. Croydon)
Role: Mrs Fox (Marcia) (episodes 13, 27, 35, 44, 55, 58, 61, 64, 66, 74, 76, 80); Lady in the Queue (episode 15)

Both Pamela's parents were in the entertainment business and she never wanted to do anything else.

Her training at the Guildhall School of Music and Drama was followed by plenty of work in rep and summer tours, as a stand-up comic. She made her TV debut in *Yes, It's the Cathode-Ray Tube Show!* in 1957 with Peter Sellers and Michael Bentine, and worked on *Jim's Inn* during the same period.

Pamela's been fortunate enough to work with all the great comics including Benny Hill and Frankie Howerd. In recent years, she's played Vi Box in three series of BBC's *Big Deal*, and Mrs Monk, the housekeeper, in *The Choir*. Still busy, particularly on stage.

Frazer champions Godfrey's cause and blackmails the minister responsible for the aerodrome project. Remembering him as the son of a chip shop owner on the Isle of Barra, he threatens to expose him to a society magazine by revealing details of his expulsion from school and sacking from a draper's shop for fingers in the till.

Godfrey's worries evaporate and life goes on at Cherry Tree Cottage.

ATTENTION!

'This episode contains one of my favourite scenes. I played a man fixing a new prefabricated door in Mainwaring's office. As I'm doing the job Mainwaring spots some holes in it which I cover up with a bit of stamp paper. When I last saw this episode, I didn't recognise myself.'
GORDON PETERS

The verger leads the Sea Scouts on their parade.

70. COME IN, YOUR TIME IS UP

Also appearing: Bill Pertwee (Chief Warden Hodges), Frank Williams (the Vicar), Edward Sinclair (the Verger), Harold Bennett (Mr Bluett), Colin Bean (Private Sponge)

While testing out their new two-man bivouac tents at weekend camp, the platoon are disturbed by Hodges dropping off the vicar, verger and the Sea Scouts, who also intend to camp. The next morning finds three German airmen in an inflatable dinghy on the lake, casualties of the previous night's raid.

With the use of a raft, Mainwaring and some of his men, together with Hodges, who's acting as interpreter, consider all ways of getting the Germans to the shore.

PIKE: Let's shoot at the rubber dinghy and sink it.
MAINWARING: We can't do that either, the bullets will go straight through and hit them. This is the penalty you pay for being a sporting nation and playing a straight bat.
WILSON: You know, it's really quite simple, sir. All we've got to do is attach a rope to the dinghy and tow it to the shore.
MAINWARING: Ah! . . . well done, Wilson . . . just wondered who'd be the first to spot that.

After the scheme fails, it's down to Pike to resolve the problem by shooting his bow and arrow to sink the dinghy.

ATTENTION!

'For the scene where the Germans are stuck in the middle of a lake in an inflatable raft, we cut a section from the bottom and replaced it with a piece of ply that was well and truly greased. When we wanted it to sink, the wood was pulled out and water rushed in at quite a rate.'
PETER DAY, Visual Effects

JEFFREY SEGAL (b. London)
Role: The Minister (episode 52); Brigadier (episode 76)

Jeffrey, always an active amateur actor, left school with plans to be a civil servant. But the war put paid to his plans, and he joined the army, serving in Italy and Germany. When a recruitment drive was launched to gather people who could help entertain the troops, Jeffrey took advantage and joined a theatrical unit.

Jeffrey, now 76, continued acting after the war and has remained busy ever since. He first worked at the Mercury Theatre, Notting Hill Gate, and various reps including Watford and Leatherhead.

Moved into TV, initially working as a back-up news commentator. Has since worked in all genres of television, including several appearances for Perry and/or Croft, in *Are You Being Served?* and *It Ain't Half Hot, Mum*. Appeared as Mr Perkins in *Rentaghost* for five years and has been seen in many other shows: *Love Hurts* (the final series), *Bergerac, Lytton's Diary* and *David Copperfield*.

On radio, he was one of the writers behind the much-loved soap *The Dales*; he made his film debut aged 13 as a schoolboy, and went on to make a handful of cameo appearances.

As well as acting, Jeffrey continues to write.

71. HIGH FINANCE

Also appearing: Bill Pertwee (Chief Warden Hodges), Frank Williams (the Vicar), Edward Sinclair (the Verger), Janet Davies (Mrs Pike), Ronnie Brody (Mr Swann), Colin Bean (Private Sponge), Natalie Kent (Miss Twelvetrees).

Jones' bank account is in the red and Mainwaring won't honour any more cheques. Mainwaring, Wilson and Pike visit Jones to sort the problem out, but the butcher's slapdash bookkeeping doesn't impress.

After failing to balance the books, Mainwaring prepares to speak to Jones at the church hall when Mr Swann, the town grocer, asks to speak urgently to Mainwaring, but he hasn't any time.

Finally it's established that the reason Jones is in the red is because the orphanage hasn't paid their bills for three months and he can't bring himself to demand payment. After further investigation a long chain of debtors is unearthed, but the buck stops with Hodges, who repays the money.

Mr Swann then reappears on the scene.

MR SWANN: I want to speak to you, Mr Mainwaring. Remember me, Swann the grocer?

MAINWARING: Oh yes, yes, yes, what is it?

MR SWANN: Well, it's a bit embarrassing in front of all these people.

MAINWARING: Your trouble is you're too sensitive, come on, spit it out.
MR SWANN: Well, I would prefer that we would go somewhere a little more private.
MAINWARING: Oh come along, be a man, tell me, tell me.
MR SWANN: Oh all right then. You're wife hasn't paid her grocery bill for six months; it comes to £49, 17 shillings and six pence, and I want it now!

Jones' butcher's shop runs into debt in *High Finance*.

72. THE FACE ON THE POSTER

Also appearing: Bill Pertwee (Chief Warden Hodges), Frank Williams (the Vicar), Edward Sinclair (the Verger). Featuring: Peter Butterworth (Mr Bugden), Harold Bennett (Mr Bluett), Gabor Vernon (the Polish Officer), Colin Bean (Private Sponge), Bill Tasker (Fred), Michael Bevis (the Police Sergeant).

Mainwaring has his heart set on becoming a major; to help him achieve his goal he's determined to turn the platoon into a company by launching a recruitment drive. A poster is designed with Jones' mug on it inviting people to join the platoon, but a mix-up at the printers finds his face plastered all over a missing POW poster issued by the police.

In the street Jones is arrested by a Polish officer and interrogated before being banished to a POW camp. The platoon's fortunes dip further when Mainwaring's vain attempts to help result in the whole platoon being thrown behind barbed wire.

JEFFREY HOLLAND (b. Walsall)
Role: Soldier (episode 75)

Jeffrey didn't contemplate acting as a career until joining an amateur company at 15. Unsure about what to do with his life, he worked at a wine merchant's straight from school, before working in the office of a cardboard box manufacturer. It was then that he decided to become an actor.

After more than four years in theatre at Coventry, small TV parts came his way. His first speaking role was a young husband in *Dixon of Dock Green*, but he also played a market stall trader in ten episodes of *Crossroads* in the mid-1970s before *Dad's Army*.

Jeffrey, who classes *Dad's Army* as his favourite programme, was offered the part of the truck-driving soldier after appearing in the stage show.

After *Dad's Army* his career blossomed and the 1980s saw him spend seven years playing Spike Dixon in *Hi-De-Hi!* and appear with Russ Abbot on his *Madhouse* shows. So far in the 1990s, he's appeared in two sitcoms, as James Twelvetrees in *You Rang, M'Lord?* and Cecil Parkin in *Oh, Doctor Beeching!*.

CHRISTMAS SPECIAL

Transmitted 26/12/75

73. MY BROTHER AND I

Also appearing: Bill Pertwee (Chief Warden Hodges), Frank Williams (the Vicar), Edward Sinclair (the Verger), Penny Irving (the Chambermaid), Arnold Diamond (the Major-General), Colin Bean (Pte Sponge).

Local Home Guard officers are throwing a sherry party for local dignitaries and Mainwaring is playing host. Jones' section act as stewards.

On the way home from Eastbourne, where he's been attending a business meeting, Frazer shares the same train compartment with Mainwaring's red-nosed, drunken brother, Barry – the black sheep of the family. He's on his way to visit George, who he hasn't seen for 15 years, to claim ownership of the pocket watch their late father owned. News that his brother is in town worries Mainwaring and he tries his utmost to keep him out of sight. But when Barry gatecrashes the sherry party, the platoon has its work cut out.

ALEX McAVOY (b. Glasgow)
Role: Sergeant (episodes 46 & 57)

Alex was a boy soprano and sang on the radio in 1944, aged 16. When he left school he wanted to be a commercial artist so trained at evening classes at Glasgow School of Art, while working during the day, first in the inspections department at a gun factory, then as a display artist for various organisations, including department stores.

Before joining the RAF for national service in 1946, Alex had begun working behind the scenes at a local theatre. Shortly after leaving the forces he studied full-time at Glasgow's drama academy.

Combined with various rep work, four years of variety and broadcasting for the BBC followed. In 1962 he left for France to study mime and movement with the world renowned Lecoq.

Alex was often cast as youngsters and during his early TV career played Sunny Boy (an 18-year-old, even though he was 45) in BBC's *Vital Spark* in 1967.

He's made a few film appearances, most notably as the teacher in Pink Floyd's *The Wall*. Remains busy today, mainly in the theatre (he was the original Jacob in *Joseph and the Amazing Technicolor Dreamcoat*). Also teaches mime and movement at a drama college in Edinburgh.

CHRISTMAS SPECIAL

Transmitted 26/12/76

74. THE LOVE OF THREE ORANGES

Also appearing: Bill Pertwee (Chief Warden Hodges), Frank Williams (the Vicar), Edward Sinclair (the Verger), Pamela Cundell (Mrs Fox), Janet Davies (Mrs Pike), Joan Cooper (Dolly), Eric Longworth (the Town Clerk), Olive Mercer (Mrs Yeatman), Colin Bean (Private Sponge).

The vicar's organised a church bazaar to raise money for the Comforts for the Troops Fund. Mainwaring sets up a committee to organise events, and selects himself as chairman, much to Hodges' annoyance.

MAINWARING: As chairman, uh, may I just bring the meeting to order and welcome all . . .
HODGES: Oi! Hold on a minute, hold on . . . why is it that whenever we have a meeting about anything, you're always the chairman? Who elected you, that's what I want to know?
MAINWARING: It was perfectly above board and legal. I was elected by the steering committee.
HODGES: And who elected the steering committee?
MAINWARING: I did!

A grim-faced Mrs Yeatman offers to run the tombola, Godfrey donates chutney and homemade wine, Jones donates a monster brawn, Mrs Fox will tell fortunes, Mrs Mainwaring will sell some of her bizarre lampshades and Hodges will auction three oranges, a scarce fruit since the war.

After another argument with his beloved, Mrs Mainwaring doesn't turn up but Pike collects her lampshades and brings them to the bazaar. In an attempt to bring peace to the Mainwaring household he's determined to acquire one of the oranges, but has to cough up ten shillings after bidding against Pike.

VERNE MORGAN
(b. Sidcup)
Role: Landord (episodes 28, 32, 55); Farmer (episode 63)

Verne always wanted to act and upon leaving school got involved in variety shows and concert parties. Primarily a comedian, he had a double-act with his wife, Betty Moore, for many years.

He was also a regular in panto before the war, during which he joined ENSA. En route to the Middle East his ship was torpedoed and he was lucky to survive.

After the war, Verne resumed his acting career and appeared in the West End as well as the occasional film. In 1953 he popped up in the *The Limping Man* as Stone, a taxi driver, and during the 1970s in two Hammer productions: *That's Your Funeral*, as a pensioner, and a records clerk in *Man at the Top*.

In addition to *Dad's Army* he had small parts in various shows including *The Best of Benny Hill* (1974) and as a butler in *Shoulder to Shoulder*, a BBC series about the suffragettes.

Verne was also a writer, penning magazine articles, numerous plays and pantomimes for local companies. He died in 1984, aged 84.

**Jones has the attention of
the platoon.**

SEASON NINE

Transmitted 2/10/77 – 13/11/77

75. WAKE-UP WALMINGTON

Also appearing: Bill Pertwee (Chief
Warden Hodges), Frank Williams (the

Alister Williamson (Bert), Michael Stainton (Frenchy).

No one seems to be taking the war seriously in Walmington so Mainwaring devises a plan for the platoon to masquerade as fifth columnists to shake everyone up a bit. With the old flour mill as their HQ, they march the country roads trying desperately to look suspicious. But whatever they do, nothing seems to shift the residents' complacency towards the Nazi threat. Finally someone reports them to the police who in turn contact the Home Guard. When Captain Square hears he sets off in pursuit.

Vicar), Edward Sinclair (the Verger), Geoffrey Lumsden (Capt. Square), Sam Kydd (the Yokel), Harold Bennett (Mr Bluett), Robert Raglan (the Colonel), Charles Hill (the Butler), Jeffrey Holland (the Soldier), Barry Linehan (the Van Driver), Colin Bean (Private Sponge),

ATTENTION!

'When I turned up to play the part, I had a driving licence but wasn't an experienced driver because I didn't own a car. I was supposed to drive this huge truck with a crash gearbox with which I was totally unfamiliar. When I got into the cab I didn't recognise any of the controls – I even had to be taught how to start the thing! With the help of the owner I struggled to drive it round this bend before nearly running over Clive Dunn. When the truck drives away and splashes Mainwaring with muddy water – which was thrown on by someone out of camera – it wasn't me at the wheel.' **JEFFREY HOLLAND**

76. THE MAKING OF PRIVATE PIKE

Bill Pertwee (Chief Warden Hodges), Frank Williams (the Vicar), Edward Sinclair (the Verger), Jean Gilpin (Sylvia), Anthony Sharp (the Colonel), Jeffrey Segal (the Brigadier), Pamela Cundell (Mrs Fox), Janet Davies (Mrs Pike), Melita Manger (Nora).

Mainwaring is soon persuaded to be an umpire during an exercise once he learns the role affords a staff car, which Hodges, who's in the church hall office at the time, can't believe.

HODGES: Staff car! How did you get a staff car?
MAINWARING: My position entitles me to one.
HODGES: Who are you kidding, your position wouldn't entitle you to a pair of roller skates.

While Pikey is drinking raspberryade at

ATTENTION!

'The scene where Pikey confides in Wilson in the staff car was originally planned for the studio. But we'd just finished lunch on location in Norfolk when David suggested we did it. We hadn't learnt the lines, or even rehearsed it, but just got on with it - two shots and that was it. The scene was a joy to do because it was beautifully written.' **IAN LAVENDER**

OLIVE MERCER (b. London)
Role: Mrs Casson (episode 13); Lady in Queue (episode 15); Mrs Yeatman (episodes 21, 44, 61, 66, 74, 77); Fierce Lady (episode 24)

After graduating from RADA, Olive worked briefly with her father before joining a rep. But in 1931 she left to marry and raise a family. While her children were growing up, she produced shows for various companies as well as local children's shows in Ruislip. Also helped set up a drama school, Mime and the Spoken Word, in the town (the most famous pupil being Russell Grant).

Didn't concentrate on acting again until her fifties, joining various reps including Watford with Jimmy Perry.

It wasn't until she was 60 that she moved into TV, clocking up a myriad of small parts, including roles in *The Forsyte Saga*, *Emergency – Ward 10*, the cleaner in *Please, Sir!*, *Doctor in the House*, *On the Buses*, an aunt in *The Likely Lads* and *Monty Python*. Regularly appeared in *Crossroads*, one of her final jobs. Worked mainly in TV – often in stern parts – but used regularly for newspaper and magazine adverts. Contracted shingles at 70 and her health never fully recovered. She died in 1983 of a heart attack.

the local cafe, Hodges niece, Sylvia, who's on leave, chats to him, and before he knows it they've arranged to go to the pictures the following evening. Sylvia takes advantage of callow Pike and they end up travelling to Eastgate in the staff car. On the way home the car runs out of petrol, and it takes Pikey all night to push the car home. It's time for Wilson to have a man to man chat with Pike.

77. KNIGHTS OF MADNESS

Bill Pertwee (Chief Warden Hodges), Frank Williams (the Vicar), Edward Sinclair (the Verger), Colin Bean (Private Sponge), Janet Davies (Mrs Pike), Olive Mercer (Mrs Yeatman), Eric Longworth (the Town Clerk), Fred McNaughton (the Mayor).

Captain Mainwaring prepares for the dragon in *Knights of Madness*.

At the 'Wings for Victory' committee meeting, plans for helping to raise money are discussed. After Mainwaring and Hodges argue it's decided that the Home Guard and wardens will share the grand finale. The platoon decides to stage the battle of Saint George and the dragon, while Hodges decides to do the samething. But he doesn't realise what Mainwaring's bunch are doing until the actual day. Not wanting to be a laughing stock, he enters the arena at the same time as the Home Guard and the battle begins.

Frazer, at the window of his undertaker's business.

78. THE MISER'S HOARD

Special Guest Appearance: Fulton Mackay (Dr McCeavedy). Also appearing: Bill Pertwee (Chief Warden Hodges), Frank Williams (the Vicar), Edward Sinclair (the Verger), Colin Bean (Pte Sponge).

Mainwaring wants to get his hands on Frazer's collection of gold sovereigns and tries persuading him to sell them and buy an annuity instead. Rumours spread around the town about the Scotsman's hoard and soon people are calling him for handouts.

Blaming Mainwaring for this sudden interest in his financial status, he's spotted taking a box to the graveyard. The platoon follow and believe they've dug up his savings, but Frazer gets the last laugh.

ATTENTION!

'By the time of *The Miser's Hoard* I'd ended up on the front row of the platoon, it was a lovely feeling. Instead of peering and smirking over Jones' shoulder, I was on the front line. It was very satisfying.'
COLIN BEAN

79. NUMBER ENGAGED

Also appearing: Bill Pertwee (Chief Warden Hodges), Frank Williams (the Vicar), Edward Sinclair (the Verger), Ronnie Brody (the GPO Man), Robert Mill (the Army Captain), Kenneth MacDonald (the Army Sergeant), Felix Bowness (the Van Driver), Colin Bean (Private Sponge), Stuart McGugan (the Scottish Sergeant), Bernice Adams (the ATS Girl).

The platoon is guarding crucial telephone wires for the weekend while the regular army enjoys a spell of leave. When the vicar and verger arrive to give an open air service, Mainwaring notices a bomb caught up in the wires.

ATTENTION!

'A stunt went wrong during *Number Engaged*. A small bomb had got lodged in the telephone wires, so the platoon commandeered a furniture van and built a tower with all the furniture. A rigid structure, it was built to fall back onto the hay and manure strategically positioned. Although I pleaded with David Croft to let me do the stunt, he refused. Just as well because when it was filmed with a stuntman, the tower collapsed and he ended up in hospital. David turned to me afterwards with his lovely wide smile, and said: "Fancy doing it now?"'

IAN LAVENDER

VICAR: Let us give thought to those things above that control our destiny. Let us raise our faces to heaven and give thanks.
MAINWARING: *(Looking up)* Good lord!
VICAR: He is indeed, Captain Mainwaring.
VERGER: *(Looking up)* Heavens above!
VICAR: I'll do the praying, Mr Yeatman.
JONES: There's a bomb in the wire, don't panic, there's a bomb in the wire.

Mainwaring decides to handle the situation and borrows furniture from a passing removal van to build a tower. After Pikey fails to dislodge the bomb, Wilson has a bright idea.

80. NEVER TOO OLD

Also appearing: Bill Pertwee (Chief Warden Hodges), Frank Williams (the Vicar), Edward Sinclair (the Verger), Pamela Cundell (Mrs Fox), Janet Davies (Mrs Pike) Colin Bean (Private Sponge), Joan Cooper (Dolly), Robert Raglan (the Colonel).

Love is in the air for Jones, who announces his marriage to Mrs Fox. In the church hall office, Mainwaring and Wilson discuss life.

MAINWARING: You know she's very well connected, Elizabeth. Her father was the suffragan bishop of Clagthorpe.
WILSON: Was he really?
MAINWARING: Led a very sheltered life, Elizabeth. *(he laughs)* Very funny. You know she hadn't even, she hadn't even

tried tomato sauce before she met me – I soon put that right.

WILSON: *(Smiling)* Marrying you must have opened up a whole new world for her.

At the ceremony, Wilson is best man, Mrs Pike Matron of Honour and Mainwaring gives the bride away. But when the Colonel phones and warns that an invasion could be imminent, the celebrations are interrupted and Jones spends his wedding night keeping guard.

The rest of the platoon arrive and decide to toast Jones' health, but not before Hodges turns up and cruelly ridicules the Home Guard.

HODGES: Look at you. What good would you be against real soldiers? Cor, dear. *(He laughs)* They'd walk straight through you. Good night. *(Mainwaring tells his men not to take any notice)*

ATTENTION!

'During this episode I marry Jones. There's a scene where Mainwaring, who gives Mrs Fox away, gets stuck between the wall and a pillar when he walks through with Mrs Fox. Well, that wasn't planned. It was during rehearsals that this first happened; Arthur thought it very funny and suggested not saying anything to anybody and doing it for the recording. The scene worked well.'
PAMELA CUNDELL

PIKE: Mr Mainwaring. Warden wasn't right was he, when he said the Nazis would walk straight through us?
MAINWARING: Of course he wasn't right.
JONES: I know one thing, they're not walking straight through me.
FRAZER: Nor me. I'll be beside you, Jonesey.
MAINWARING: We'll all be beside you, Jonesey. We'll stick together, you can rely on that. Anybody tries to take our homes or our freedom away from us, they'll

find out what we can do. We'll fight. And we're not alone, there are thousands of us all over England.

FRAZER: And Scotland.

MAINWARING: And Scotland. All over Great Britain, in fact. Men who'll stand together when their country needs them.

WILSON: Excuse me, sir. Don't you think it might be a nice idea if we paid our tribute to them?

MAINWARING: For once, Wilson, I agree with you. *(They raise their mugs)* To Britain's Home Guard.

ALL: To Britain's Home Guard.

CHRISTMAS NIGHT WITH THE STARS

A number of *Dad's Army* sketches were recorded over the years, including *Broadcast To The Empire* in 1972. In this 15-minute sketch, Mainwaring and his men are taking part in the radio programme *To Absent Friends*, sending greetings to the troops all over the Empire, just before the King's speech.

After rehearsing their lines and simulating sound effects they discover their moment of fame has been cancelled – the schedule has fallen behind and the feature has been dropped.

Wilson does his best man duties at the wedding of Jack Jones and Marcia Fox.

THE CREDITS

THE MAIN CAST

ARTHUR LOWE: Captain Mainwaring
JOHN LE MESURIER: Sergeant Wilson
CLIVE DUNN: Lance Corporal Jones
JOHN LAURIE: Private Frazer
JAMES BECK: Private Walker (episode 59 last episode before death)
ARNOLD RIDLEY: Private Godfrey
IAN LAVENDER: Private Pike

PRODUCTION TEAM

Series created by Jimmy Perry & David Croft.

SCRIPTS BY: Jimmy Perry & David Croft.

SIGNATURE TUNE: Words by Jimmy Perry.
Music by Jimmy Perry and Derek Taverner. Sung by Bud Flanagan.

CLOSING THEME: Band of the Coldstream Guards conducted by their Director of Music, Captain Trevor L Sharpe, M.B.E., L.R.A.M., A.R.C.M., p.s.m.

COSTUMES: George Ward (series 1 & 4); Odette Barrow (series 3); Michael Burdle (series 3); Barbara Kronig (series 4); Judy Allen (episode 40); Susan Wheal (series 5–7); Mary Husband (series 8 & 9, episodes 73 & 74).

MAKE-UP: Sandra Exelby (series 1); Cecile Hay-Arthur (series 3); Cynthia Goodwin (series 4 & 5); Penny Bell (episode 40); Anna Chesterman (series 5 & 6); Ann Ailes (series 6); Sylvia Thornton (series 7–9, episode 73 & 74).

VISUAL EFFECTS: Peter Day (series 3–6 & 8); John Friedlander (series 4); Ron Oates (series 4); Len Hutton (episode 40); Tony Harding (series 5); Jim Ward (series 7); Martin Gutteridge (series 9).

LIGHTING: George Summers (series 1, 2, 4); Howard King (series 3–9, episodes 40, 73 & 74).

STUDIO SOUND: James Cole (series 1 & 2); Michael McCarthy (series 3–8, episode 74); John Holmes (series 3 & 4); John Delany (series 5); Alan Machin (series 8, episode 73); Laurie Taylor (series 9).

FILM CAMERAMAN: James Balfour (series 3, 5 & 6); Stewart A. Farnell (series 4 & 5); Len Newson (series 7); Peter Chapman (series 8 & 9).

FILM SOUND: Les Collins (series 4 & 5, episode 40); Ron Blight (series 5) John Gatland (series 6 & 7); Bill Chesneau (series 8); Graham Bedwell (series 9).

FILM EDITOR: Bob Rymer (series 3, 5 & 6, episode 40); Bill Harris (series 4–7); John Stothart (series 8); John Dunstan (series 9).

PRODUCTION ASSISTANTS: Bob Spiers (series 7); Jo Austin (series 8, episodes 73 & 74); Gordon Elsbury (series 9).

DESIGN: Alan Hunter-Craig (series 1); Paul Joel (series 1–6, episode 40); Oliver Bayldon (series 2); Ray London (series 3); Richard Hunt (series 3); Bryan Ellis (series 7); Robert Berk (series 8, episode 73); Geoff Powell (series 9); Tim Gleeson (series 9).

DIRECTOR: Harold Snoad and Bob Spiers directed certain episodes, the rest were directed by David Croft.

PRODUCER: David Croft.

JIMMY BECK

Joe Walker's the local spiv trading in everything from whisky to women's silks. Classing himself as a wholesale supplier and scrap dealer, he's dodged enlistment on the pretence that his work qualifies as a reserved occupation. When he did get called up, he was swiftly discharged for being allergic to corned beef.

Although outspoken, a Casanova around Walmington and a black market trader, Walker also shows altruistic qualities. When Godfrey was cold-shouldered by everyone after admitting that he was a conscientious objector, Walker was the only one who openly revealed sympathy for the old man. Behind the flashy facade is a genuinely warmhearted guy.

Private Walker was one of the most popular characters in *Dad's Army*, and consequently Jimmy Beck – who wore a false moustache for the series – was frequently spotted in the street by admiring fans. His widow, Kay, recalls visiting the local market one Christmas. 'We were buying some holly and mistletoe and passed a barrelman doing his spiel. He suddenly saw Jimmy, and shouted: "Hey, you should be doing this!" Jimmy told him that he worked from a script and couldn't possibly do it.

'The funny thing was that as long as we were there, the trader was unable to do it because he felt embarrassed that Jimmy could probably do it better.'

Born in Islington, London in 1929, Jimmy was educated at Popham Elementary School. His childhood was tough: while his mother made artificial flowers for a meagre fee, his father spent long periods unemployed.

From the age of 14, Jimmy attended art school for three years. After graduating he worked as a commercial artist until being called up for national service. Upon leaving military life, he pursued a career not in art but in the theatre.

His theatrical break arrived when he was employed as a student actor earning £1 a week, at a rep in Margate in the early 1950s. Stints at various reps, including Hornchurch, Ipswich and Scarborough followed before he joined York, first as ASM, then progressing to leading roles in productions like *The Entertainer* and *The Merchant of Venice*.

While working at York, Jimmy met his wife, Kay. 'I had recently separated from my first husband and was taking a holiday in the area. The owners of the farm next to where I was staying were hosting a

party and Jimmy had been invited. We saw each other every day from that first meeting – it was very romantic,' smiles Kay. 'Jimmy frequently cycled the ten miles to see me – and sometimes after the evening show!'

Caroline Dowdeswell, who appeared in the first series of *Dad's Army* as Miss King, was ASM at York in 1963, when Jimmy played in *The Merchant of Venice*. She was very impressed with his performance. 'Everyone thought he was the finest Shylock they had seen. I was on the prompt book and remember sobbing my heart out during rehearsals as he gave a truly poignant performance.'

Jimmy began receiving rave reviews about his performances in rep and realised that if he wanted

The Casanova of Walmington in action.

CAROLINE DOWDESWELL
(b. Oldham)
Role: Janet King (episodes 1, 2, 3, 4, 6)

Caroline, whose grandparents were actors, knew from an early age it was the life for her. At the age of 12 she attended theatre school for four years and joined her first company, Bromley Rep, aged 17, moving to York a year later.

After appearing in *Dad's Army*, Caroline made a good living out of acting for a further ten years until retiring from the profession in 1978, due to ill health. She'd worked mainly on TV, presenting the Sunday evening religious programme, *Friends and Neighbours*, appearing as Thora Hird's daughter in two series of *Ours is a Nice House*, *Softly Softly*, *Redcap* and six months in *Crossroads* as Ann Taylor, David Hunter's secretary and love interest.

Also seen in numerous sitcoms such as *Man About the House*, as Richard O'Sullivan's girlfriend, and *Billy Liar*.

Caroline is now a partner in a publishing company, often travelling the world on business.

to progress in the business, London was the place to be. By now Kay and Jimmy had married, and they decided to make the move.

After settling into suitable accommodation, the Becks took in a lodger. Jean Alexander—best known for playing Hilda Ogden in *Coronation Street* – had worked with Jimmy at York, and when she wanted to try her luck in the capital, Jimmy and Kay put her up.

'I was at York between 1958 and 1961 when Jimmy was there,' says Jean. 'He was great to work with, an extremely fine performer. He was good in straight plays as well as comedies, especially *The Long, the Short and the Tall*. We even appeared together in a children's TV show called *Television Club*.'

Jean was particularly impressed with his portrayal of Walker. 'It was the little details that helped make it such a great character: the shrugging of the shoulders, cigarette hanging from the side of his mouth – typical of the spivvy type of the time.'

Jimmy was grateful for the opportunity to join *Dad's Army*, but Kay admits that he was sometimes disappointed with the character's scope. 'When he looked at the scripts, he found he didn't have a lot to do. And that can be very frustrating, but he still enjoyed it.'

From the start, Jimmy helped shape Walker's personality. 'He actually liked the spiv types around at that time,' explains Kay, 'and knew their kindness. Even though they might appear rough and ready, great camaraderie existed between them – he wanted this to come out in the character.'

The exposure gained from appearing in a top comedy series like *Dad's Army* was immense and it wasn't long before offers for other TV roles began arriving. Other appearances on the small screen included parts in *Z Cars, Softly, Softly, The Troubleshooters, Coronation Street* (playing Sergeant Bowden in 1964) and even *Jackanory*. At the time, Jimmy told a reporter on the *Sunday Post:* 'If you're asked to do one it means you have arrived as an actor. Everybody wants to get on it.'

The most notable offer of work was the lead role in LWT's *Romany Jones*. Jimmy played workshy Bert Jones in two series of the programme. Producing the show was Stuart Allen. 'I was very fond of Jimmy and he was in my first production, *The Bishop Rides Again*, in 1966, the pilot of *All Gas and Gaiters*. Jimmy played a lot of policemen in those days, and that's what he was in the pilot.

'We did a few things together but *Romany Jones* was the biggest. Jimmy had a great sense of humour and was so likeable. It was his charm that endeared him to people and this came across in *Romany Jones*.

Jimmy died in 1973; he was 44. His last transmitted episode was *Things That Go Bump In The Night*. Studio work on *The Honourable Man* contained the actual last scenes he shot.

While opening a fete in aid of dogs for the blind he suddenly felt ill. 'He had this awful pain, so we left the fete and went home,' says Kay. 'I called the doctor and within an hour he was being rushed to hospital. I wanted a specialist to see Jimmy but it seemed none were available.

'Not knowing what to do, I called Arthur Lowe who was wonderful. He said: "Leave it to me." And he arranged for a specialist to see Jimmy – for that I'll always be grateful.'

While Jimmy was unconscious in hospital, an update on his condition was pinned on the rehearsal room noticeboard for all the cast to see.

Walker takes a bath.

Jimmy Beck's premature death
deeply affected the cast.

KENNETH MACDONALD
(b. Manchester)
Role: Army Sergeant (episode 79)

Kenneth — whose father was a professional wrestler — had already become a well-known face on TV by the time he appeared in *Dad's Army*: for seven years he was Gunner Nobby Clark in *It Ain't Half Hot, Mum*.

He turned to acting straight from school, with his first job at Leatherhead. After years of rep and theatre he made his TV debut as a villain in *Z Cars*. He has worked in plenty of TV shows, including 13 years as Mike the landlord in *Only Fools and Horses* and a stint in *Brookside*.

Still busy in the theatre and on TV — he's just finished filming a new drama series for Anglia.

For a while Ian wondered whether the series could survive the death of Jimmy Beck. 'It was such a team effort, losing such a favourite character seemed an impossible thing, but it survived.'

To help fill the void left behind by Jimmy's untimely death, a new character — Mr Cheeseman, played by Welsh actor Talfryn Thomas — was drafted in to the platoon. 'I thought it was a bit of inspired writing but it didn't quite work and the character was dropped,' says Ian Lavender.

One thing is for sure: Jimmy Perry and David Croft could never have replaced the wonderful character of Walker. But with the demise of the irreverent crook, a sizeable thorn in Mainwaring's side was sadly lost.

Jimmy lived for a further three weeks. 'He was operated on for a suspected ulcer but during the operation his pancreas burst. In those days there was nothing that could be done,' says Kay.,

A couple of days after Jimmy's death, a young boy came knocking on Kay's door. 'He asked for Jimmy's autograph. I told him he'd died, to which the boy said: "Yes, I know, but could I have his autograph?" He was so young he just didn't understand that Jimmy wasn't around anymore.'

When it came to filming the seventh season in 1974, the first since Jimmy's death, there was a cloud of sadness hanging over the affair. Ian Lavender recalls: 'It was very odd without Jimmy; we stopped doing lots of silly little things. Often when we were standing around waiting to shoot a scene on location we'd have a bit of a singsong.

'There were several good voices in the platoon and we'd all have a go harmonising while Arthur Lowe conducted. Somebody started doing it while we were waiting to shoot the first episode of that series and no one joined in. It just didn't seem right.'

CROFT ON BECK
We realised that all was not well with Jimmy Beck's health while on location filming for his last series. However, he soldiered on until we arrived at the studio on Sunday 22 July 1973 for the recording of *The Recruit* to learn that he'd been taken to hospital. Jimmy Perry and I ran quickly through the script to see if the show could go on without Jimmy Beck's studio appearance. We had scenes in which he appeared on film and decided that when it came to the parade scene, a note would be left in his place saying that he had gone 'To the Smoke', which was the Cockney way of saying London. At that stage we hoped that Jimmy would return in time for the next series but he died about three weeks later. Jimmy's 'Walker' was a lovely character and we decided that he made a unique contribution to the programme and could not be replaced.

BILL PERTWEE

CHIEF WARDEN HODGES

William 'Put that light out!' Hodges runs a greengrocer's in Walmington's high street by day, and pesters Captain Mainwaring, who he calls Napoleon, by night when performing his nocturnal duties as the town's Chief Warden.

Donning the familiar white helmet, Hodges has let the newly acquired power of being chief warden go to his head. On a personal crusade to challenge Mainwaring's higher status in the town, Hodges will do anything to get one over on the portly bank manager.

Over the years Bill Pertwee has been given plenty of advice but one piece from producer David Croft is particularly valuable. 'David said to me one day: "If you're afraid of failure, you're never going to be a success." And of course he was right.'

The advice was apposite for Bill because his tenacity duly rewarded him with a varied career in entertainment that began in earnest when Beryl Reid accepted some of his comedy material for a London revue. As a result, he was later invited to join the company, turning professional some months later.

But before entering the world of showbiz, Bill

held down a number of jobs, including making parts for Spitfires, window-cleaning and being assistant baggage boy to the Indian cricket team in 1946.

Born in 1926 in Amersham, Buckinghamshire, Bill experienced a precarious early education and was unable to write even his own name accurately until he was 12. But after moving to a small private school where learning became fun, Bill's education was quickly back on track.

When war broke out in 1939, he was evacuated to Sussex, a part of the country he's grown to love. 'It's beautiful. I got my first taste of real countryside there at the impressionable age of 12. I learnt to fish on the River Arun and during the war years set up a dating agency with some mates. The Canadian Army was billeted all over the region, and we'd fix the officers up with the posh ladies of the village while the privates and corporals went out with the local girls,' smiles Bill. 'For fixing them up we'd get little treats in return like a tin of ham or chocolates.'

At 16, Bill left school in search of work. Until he broke in to the entertainment business in 1954, some 12 years later, he experienced a chequered career encompassing numerous jobs.

In the 1950s, Bill spent time with various

acting groups, and when the offer to help his cousin, the late Jon Pertwee – alias Doctor Who, on a variety tour came along, he jumped at the chance, even though it involved no actual acting.

When the tour finished, Bill found employment at a school outfitters in London. One day he received a phone call from Ronnie Hill that was to change his life. The producer's invitation led to Bill joining Beryl Reid's revue at the Watergate Theatre.

For eight weeks, Bill continued working at the outfitters during the day while doing the revue in the evenings. But by 1955 he knew he wanted to act professionally and settled down to concentrate on his future career.

A memory that's indelibly etched on his mind is his first professional summer season

engagement. For two weeks the small acting company played at Bognor Regis before moving to Gorleston on Sea, near Great Yarmouth, for the main season. Bill recalls: 'It was only a little show and I was terribly green and doing everything wrong – or so it seemed.

'There were only about eight of us in the company so it was incredibly hard work, but I loved every minute. By the end of the season I'd learnt so much about the profession. It was a marvellous time and a wonderful summer. In my spare time I played cricket, went swimming and remember thinking that this was what entertainment was all about – it was magic.'

As the years passed, Bill kept busy with radio, small TV parts and plenty of variety seasons. The 1950s closed in style with an offer to join the second series of radio's popular weekly comedy show, *Beyond Our Ken,* with Kenneth Williams and Kenneth Horne among the cast. Soon after the show finished in 1964, Bill was recruited for the equally funny *Round the Horne.*

Although Bill Pertwee has never made it to star billing status in the entertainment world, he's become a well-respected and versatile performer, moving between media with ease.

In 1967 he was offered a couple of lines in an episode of *Hugh and I,* a BBC sitcom produced by David Croft. Working for Croft in this one-off episode proved advantageous because a year later he was given a few lines as an air raid warden in *Dad's Army.* The character of Hodges appeared again in the fourth episode. From that moment the part expanded into a regular character, who was constantly needling Mainwaring.

Bill has only fond memories of playing Hodges in *Dad's Army.* 'I'll always remember the early morning coach trip from the hotel to where we

MAVIS PUGH (b. Kent)
Role: Lady Maltby (episode 65)

Mavis' appearance as the haughty Lady Maltby, who donates her Rolls-Royce to the Walmington Home Guard, was her first job on TV.

As a child Mavis was a keen dancer and fond of literature so her choice to study drama at Oxford's International School upon leaving boarding school came as no surprise to her family.

Until making her TV debut in the 1970s, she spent many years in rep and theatre productions around the country. Began her career at rep in West Hartlepool before spells at other theatres followed, including Watford with Jimmy Perry. Her first West End appearance was in *Little Women* at the Westminster Theatre.

Since *Dad's Army* she's appeared in many TV shows, mainly comedies, including an episode of *Fawlty Towers, Spooner's Patch, It Ain't Half Hot, Mum* and *You Rang, M'Lord?*

Her film appearances include an expletive-spouting teacher in *A Class of Miss McMichael* with Glenda Jackson in 1978 and the third *Pink Panther* movie.

Mavis is still acting and does a lot of TV commercials.

Hodges in fancy dress.

filmed the battle scenes,' he says. 'It was only three or four miles and the countryside was beautiful. The weather was always good. We had nothing but sunshine for our filming; in all the years we went there, we only had three days of rain and one day of snow.

'It's extraordinary. I've been to places all over the British Isles and people will come up and talk to me about *Dad's Army*. I was in a small Scottish village once and I visited the only shop to buy a postcard. As I went out, this lady followed me. She said: "Oh, I've got to talk to you. You're from *Dad's Army*, I can't believe it – what are you doing here?" By the time I'd finished speaking to her a crowd of villagers had gathered round.'

Since the series finished Bill has continued with theatre work – he toured as Sergeant Beetroot, the Crowman's assistant in *Worzel Gummidge* – pantomimes and TV, including the role of Police Constable Wilson in Perry and Croft's *You Rang, M'Lord?*

As well as the glorious memories of being associated with such a classic sitcom as *Dad's Army*, Bill and other members of the cast have been able to use the show as a vehicle for helping to raise money for charity.

Whenever the programme is picked as the theme for a charity function, it's always a resounding success. 'People go mad and won't let us go. They know all the lines, the episodes and often things many of the cast have forgotten. The affection for the programme is unbelievable.'

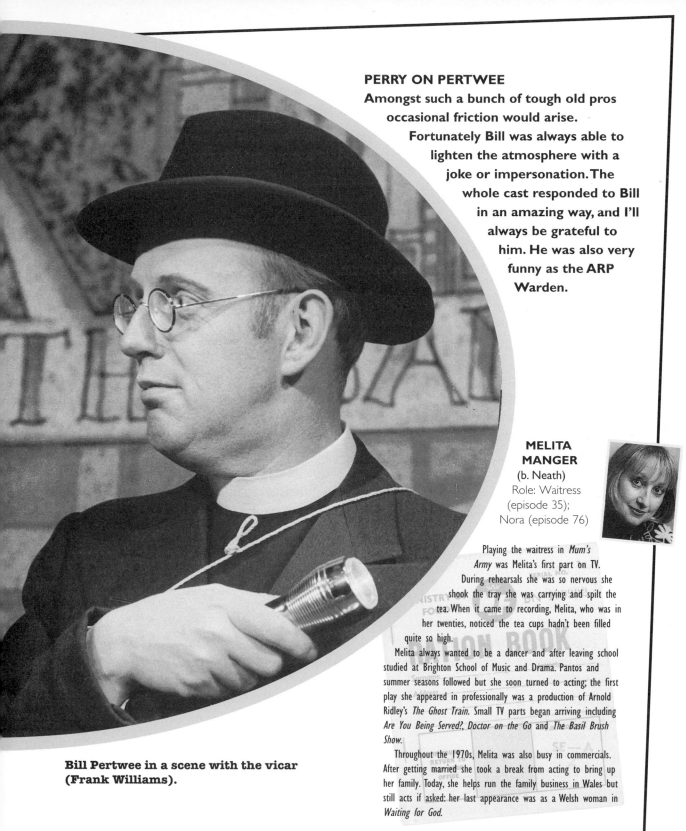

PERRY ON PERTWEE

Amongst such a bunch of tough old pros occasional friction would arise. Fortunately Bill was always able to lighten the atmosphere with a joke or impersonation. The whole cast responded to Bill in an amazing way, and I'll always be grateful to him. He was also very funny as the ARP Warden.

Bill Pertwee in a scene with the vicar (Frank Williams).

MELITA MANGER
(b. Neath)
Role: Waitress (episode 35); Nora (episode 76)

Playing the waitress in *Mum's Army* was Melita's first part on TV. During rehearsals she was so nervous she shook the tray she was carrying and spilt the tea. When it came to recording, Melita, who was in her twenties, noticed the tea cups hadn't been filled quite so high.

Melita always wanted to be a dancer and after leaving school studied at Brighton School of Music and Drama. Pantos and summer seasons followed but she soon turned to acting; the first play she appeared in professionally was a production of Arnold Ridley's *The Ghost Train*. Small TV parts began arriving including *Are You Being Served?*, *Doctor on the Go* and *The Basil Brush Show*.

Throughout the 1970s, Melita was also busy in commercials. After getting married she took a break from acting to bring up her family. Today, she helps run the family business in Wales but still acts if asked: her last appearance was as a Welsh woman in *Waiting for God*.

Dad's Army: The Movie

Filmed on location and at Shepperton Studios, England. A Norcon Production for Columbia Pictures. Released in 1971.

MAIN CAST
Arthur Lowe (Capt. Mainwaring)
John Le Mesurier (Sgt. Wilson)
Clive Dunn (Lance Cpl. Jones)
John Laurie (Pte. Frazer)
James Beck (Pte. Walker)
Arnold Ridley (Pte. Godfrey)
Ian Lavender (Pte. Pike)

SUPPORTING CAST
Liz Frazer (Mrs Pike)
Bernard Archard (Major General Fullard)
Derek Newark (R.S.M.)
Bill Pertwee (Hodges)
Frank Williams (Vicar)
Edward Sinclair (Verger)
Anthony Sagar (Police Sgt.)
Pat Coombs (Mrs Hall)
Roger Maxwell (Peppery Old Gent)
Paul Dawkins (Nazi General)
Sam Kydd (Nazi Orderly)
Michael Knowles (Staff Capt.)
Fred Griffiths (Bert King)
John Baskcomb (Mayor)
Alvar Lidell (Newsreader)
George Roubicek (German Radio Operator)
Scott Fredericks (Nazi Photographer)

Ingo Mogendorf (Nazi Pilot)
Franz Van Norde (Nazi Co-Pilot)
John Henderson (Radio Shop Assistant)
Harriet Rhys (Girl in Bank)
Dervis Ward (AA Man)
Robert Raglan (Inspector Hardcastle)
John D. Collins (Naval Officer)
Alan Haines (Marine Officer)

THE PLATOON
Desmond Cullum-Jones, Frank Godfrey, Freddie White, David Fennell, George Hancock, Colin Bean, Freddie Wiles, Leslie Noyes, Hugh Hastings, Bernard Severn.

PRODUCTION CREDITS
Music composed and conducted by Wilfred Burns
Screenplay: Jimmy Perry and David Croft
Producer: John R Sloan
Director: Norman Cohen

When Jimmy Perry and David Croft developed an idea for a big screen version of *Dad's Army*, they secured the help of Norman Cohen, who later directed the film, to hawk a synopsis around the industry's moguls. After a few rejections, Cohen sent the proposal to executives at Columbia Pictures who snapped it up. 'There wouldn't have been a film without

Norman,' admits David Croft. 'Jimmy and I knew he was an entrepreneur and he offered us a £500 advance to find a film production company.'

The extra funds pumped in to the big screen production meant many financial restrictions associated with the TV product were lifted. The streets of Walmington-on-Sea were no longer deserted as, thanks to the hiring of extras, the seaside town's population soared overnight. A bigger budget also

John Laurie, in suitable expression for an undertaker.

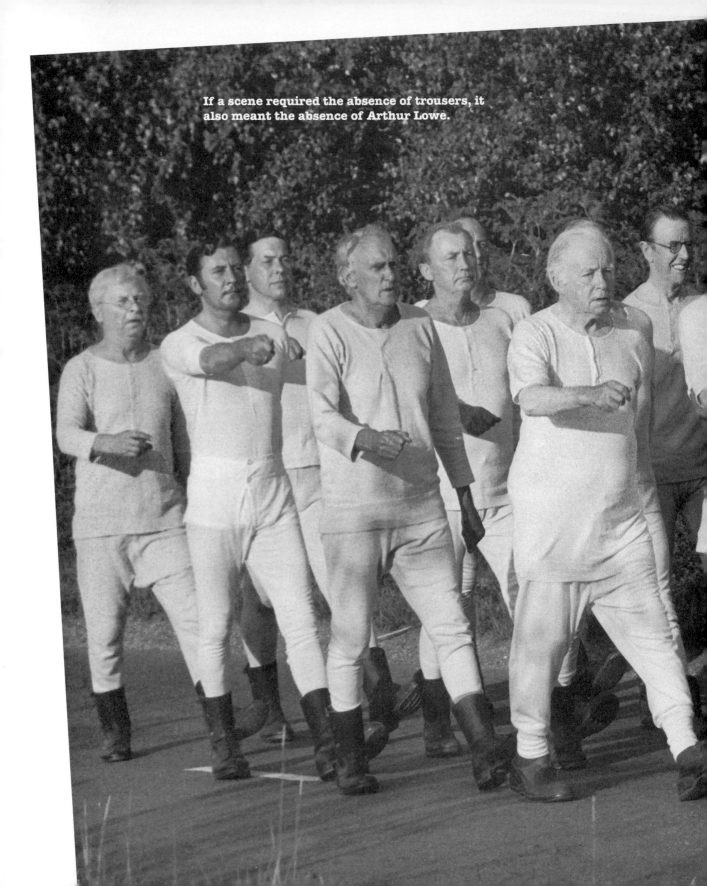

If a scene required the absence of trousers, it also meant the absence of Arthur Lowe.

meant more footage was taken on location, and there was less reliance on interior shots, very much a trademark of its small screen relation.

Many people believe the more expansive style of the movie created by the injection of cash diluted the close-knit atmosphere one had come to expect and love in *Dad's Army*.

Changes were made including renaming the bank Martin's instead of Swallow. Jimmy explains the reason: 'I was responsible for this alteration. When the TV series started Martin's Bank existed so I changed the name to Swallow. But by the time the film was made, I believe Martin's had gone so the name could be used.'

A disappointing factor for many fans of the TV show was the absence of Janet Davies as Mrs Pike, a role she had already made her own on TV. The part of the overprotective mother was given to comedy actress Liz Fraser – famous for her appearances in the *Carry On!* series – instead.

'I don't think the recasting worked in the audiences' eyes,' says Jimmy Perry. 'It was a mistake, in my view, not to cast Janet in the role because the viewing public had come to recognise her as Mrs Pike. But that was a decision taken by Columbia.'

Janet's son, Andrew Gardiner, recalls how this affected his mother. 'I think the production company wanted a bigger name as far as the film world was concerned, but being dropped from the movie hit my mother hard because she'd done so many TV episodes.'

One person who didn't feel the film worked well was Ian Lavender. 'There was one major mistake: we saw the Germans. It would have been better if we'd never actually seen the reality of what Mainwaring and his platoon were up against. Although we occasionally saw glimpses of them in the TV series, it wasn't anything like what we saw in the film.

Sadly, Jimmy Perry was also not entirely happy with how the film turned out. 'The power for making decisions was taken out of our hands; David was in Australia for a time, and although I worked on the film, it was only as technical advisor. There were many arguments because Columbia didn't want what we'd conceived, and, in my view, the whole set-up was wrong – it couldn't capture the atmosphere of the TV series.'

Once the production responsibilities for making the movie left the hands of Perry and Croft, change was inevitable. Fresh faces bring their own ideas and points of view, and even though many people weren't enthused by the film at the time of release, it has survived the test of time admirably. Unlike many other sitcom offshoots, the big screen version of Dad's Army retains its timeless humour and high production values, 26 years on.

For one actor in particular, the opening scenes always brings back memories. Colin Bean – who played Private Sponge, one of the stalwarts of the platoon's back row – had been in an original shot but when it was decided to reshoot, his scene ended up on the cutting-room floor. Colin explains: 'One of the early scenes showed me walking down the high street while Jimmy Beck was walking up. After stopping, we both looked across the road at Mainwaring and all the men marching along.

'Jimmy asked me: "'Ere, what's ole Mainwaring getting up to?" I replied: "I don't know." When the film came out this scene had been refilmed to serve as an introduction for the vicar. As Walker walks up the street it's the vicar he meets, not me.'

Whenever it's repeated, the film always receives a good write-up, but David Croft, like his co-writer, wasn't pleased with the outcome. 'I'm not sure that the director really knew where the show was coming from. And I think the cast detected that the film wasn't going as well as it might. Last time it was on TV I sat down to watch, but after about three quarters of an hour I switched off. It contained some funny sequences but just lost the spirit of the TV series.'

As with the TV series, the film's release was greeted with mixed reviews by the Press. While a critic at *The Times* said it was 'played in the best traditions of national farce', the *Daily Express* stated: 'The familiar characters of the successful television series march over well-trodden ground and never plant a boot in new territory.' Meanwhile the *Evening Standard* felt 'it seems a bit slow and stiff in the limbs'.

But despite the Press's cool reception, the film was popular enough among cinema audiences to justify discussions taking place concerning a sequel. Entitled *Dad's Army and the Secret U-boat Base*, the film was to focus on a small Welsh coastal town. After several warships are sunk in the immediate waters, Mainwaring and his men are sent to

ATTENTION!

Look out for the scene where the marching platoon change from civvies down to long johns before going into military uniforms. Arthur Lowe is missing because of a clause in his contract stopping him having to take part in scenes that involved removing his trousers!

investigate. Eventually a secret underwater submarine base is discovered and Mainwaring and his platoon are fundamental in eliminating the threat. An outline was prepared by Jimmy Perry and David Croft but the project never materialised.

EDWARD EVANS (b. London)
Role: Mr Reed (episode 9); Mr Rees (episode 19); General Monteverdi (episode 31)

Both Edward's parents were actors but he didn't follow in their footsteps immediately. After working in advertising and training as a pub cellarman, he secured some work in the late 1920s as a stuntman in films; this led to small parts and crowd work.

During the war, Edward, who speaks fluent Italian, served in Italy. He later used his language skills playing several Italian characters, such as General Monteverdi.

After the war his big screen career began in earnest. He's since made over 30 films, among them *The Small Voice*, *The Man Upstairs* and *Till Death Us Do Part* (he also appeared in the TV series).

On TV he spent eight months of 1965 in *Coronation Street* as Lionel Petty, who bought the corner shop from Florrie Lindley. Also seen in many episodes of *Compact*. His TV highlight was playing Bob Grove between 1954 and 1957 in BBC's first soap, *The Grove Family*. Edward, who's now 82, has retired from acting.

EDWARD SINCLAIR

MAURICE YEATMAN

Maurice Yeatman is Verger of St Aldhelms, Walmington-on-Sea, as well as leader of the town's Sea Scouts. Frazer once compared his crumpled face to 'a sour prune'. Always fawning on the Vicar, Yeatman, who's married to Anthea, is forever snitching, usually at Mainwaring's expense, particularly when accidents occur at the church hall. A rather untrusting sort of chap, Yeatman, one of twins, is something of a gossip.

Edward, a Mancunian, was born into a theatrical family in 1914. His father was a stage actor, while his mother danced and sang. So it's no surprise to hear that they introduced their son to the stage at an early age – he was six months old when he was carried on in *The Midnight Mail.*

When his father died, Edward was only 14. With two other children to support, his mother couldn't afford to let him attend drama school. By this time the family was living in Kingston-upon-Thames, Surrey. If he couldn't train professionally, the next best thing was to work on an amateur basis, and before the outbreak of war Edward had joined a local amateur company.

It wasn't long before he was producing, directing and playing lead parts in various productions, including *Busman's Honeymoon* and *The Admirable Crichton*. Edward loved every minute of it, as his widow, Gladys Sinclair, confirms. 'He was keen on writing lyrics and wrote lots of things for the theatre club, without a doubt acting was in his blood. When I first knew him, I could quickly tell he loved it. Every free moment seemed to be spent at rehearsals or giving performances.'

When he was called up, he joined the Army and became involved with concert parties for the troops. A record of ill health meant Edward was based in this country during the hostilities. 'At the age of six months, he'd been desperately ill with a bronchial condition, and for a time his parents feared he was going to die,' says Gladys, who married Edward in 1940.

For the rest of his life, Edward was a bronchitic although he disguised the fact well. 'The only way it revealed itself was that he puffed and panted a lot,' she says, 'but then often the parts he took were usually heavy character roles which required him to puff and pant!'

When Edward was demobbed in 1945, he resumed his amateur acting career. Even though he enjoyed acting, he resisted the temptation to turn professional, realising the insecurity of the profession was incompatible with the responsibilities of a married man, who by this time was soon to become a father. His one desire was to support his family and the most secure route was the one he knew: selling. From the age of 17, Edward had worked as a salesman, first selling men's clothing in a Kingston shop before moving to a high class store in London.

'It wasn't the best job for his bronchial condition because of all the fluff from the clothing,' admits Gladys. 'When he came out of the army, he vowed never to return to selling clothes; but with a young family to support he needed to do something in the same field and ended up selling hairdressing chairs to local salons.'

Once his two sons, Peter and Keith, were in their teens and nearing the end of their education, Edward – then in his late forties – finally decided it was time to chance his luck in

the precarious world of professional acting. He first started working in radio before offers for TV came along, including the role of Barkis in the serial *David Copperfield*, *Z Cars*, *Special Branch* and *Doctor Finlay's Casebook*. As well as the *Dad's*

CARMEN SILVERA (b. Toronto)
Role: Mrs Gray (episode 35)i

Carmen, best known as Edith in BBC's hit comedy *'Allo, 'Allo*, appeared in the rather moving episode *Mum's Army* as a woman who experiences a brief encounter with Mainwaring.

Although she's forged a successful career for herself in acting, Carmen originally wanted to be a dancer. Upon settling in England, she trained in ballet from the age of three. When evacuated to Montreal during the war she was given the opportunity to attend lessons with the Ballet Russé, later appearing in three of their shows.

But when the war finished she returned to England and turned her attention to acting; she enrolled at LAMDA before beginning her career in rep.

Carmen made her TV debut in *Z Cars* before landing the prominent role of Camilla Hope in BBC's 1960s drama *Compact*. Among her many TV credits are appearances in *New Scotland Yard*, *Dr Who*, *Within These Walls* and *The Gentle Touch*. She's also been seen in *The Generation Game* and *What's My Line*.

On stage, Carmen has appeared in many West End productions including *Waters of the Moon* with Ingrid Bergman and *Hobson's Choice* with Penelope Keith. She recently appeared as Georgette in *School for Wives*.

Army movie, he can be seen as a taxi driver in the 1973 film, *No Sex Please, We're British*.

But it's for his perfectly crafted performance as the verger in *Dad's Army* that he is remembered. Edward actually first appeared as the caretaker in the fifth episode, *The Showing Up Of Corporal Jones*. He was then cast in the occasional episode, but it wasn't until the fifth season (1972) that he became a regular, by which time he was billed as the verger. 'It was only a small part at first,' says Gladys, 'but Teddy was delighted to be offered it.'

As the show progressed the number of lines Edward was allocated increased, and he loved the part. 'The role was wonderful for him,

Edward Sinclair, in trouble in the *Dad's Army* movie.

Edward Sinclair with Arthur Lowe and
John Le Mesurier.

definitely the highlight of his career.

'Just as the series finished he'd started
receiving offers to play panto, and if he'd lived
long enough his career would have prospered
thanks to *Dad's Army*.' Sadly, that was not to be.
Edward's devotion to his family meant that he
started his acting comparatively late, and as a
result was just reaching the peak of his career
when he died of a heart attack.

CROFT ON SINCLAIR

**To drive with Teddy Sinclair was an
experience more terrifying than Magic
Mountain in Disneyland! He was always a
courteous and polite person and to him,
having a conversation with someone
without actually looking them in the face
was not to be countenanced. Having sat
next to him in his car I found this habit
worrying enough. Thinking to counter this**
**idiosyncrasy by sitting behind him, imagine
my horror when he continually turned
round in his seat to talk to me head on. The
gentle protests by Frank Williams with the
words: 'Teddy, Teddy, look where you're
going!' were to no avail. I never travelled
with him again.**

AVRIL ANGERS (b. Liverpool)
Role: Telephone Operator
(episodes 15 & 33)

Avril, born of theatrical parents, never felt
stagestruck but pursued a career in the entertainment
world because it seemed the logical thing to do. She
made her debut as a dancer at the age of 14.

Went on to write her own material for a stand-up comedy
routine before moving into TV. Had her own series *Dear Dotty*, but
also seen in *All Creatures Great and Small*, *Coronation Street* (in two
different roles), *The Dustbinmen* and *Just Liz*. Avril appeared with
Arthur Lowe in the 1970 series *The More We Are Together*.

Avril is still busy in TV, recently filming an episode of *Victoria and
Albert* for Granada. Her extensive theatrical performances include
many West End appearances in *Oklahoma!*

173

FRANK WILLIAMS

Bespectacled Reverend Timothy Farthing is Vicar of St Aldhelms, Walmington-on-Sea. Ineffectual and rather huffy at times, Farthing – who's partial to the odd double whisky – is regularly in dispute with Captain Mainwaring over life-threatening issues such as whose turn it is to use the church hall. Before arriving at the sleepy seaside resort, Farthing's life involved working abroad as a missionary.

Two years ago, Frank met someone who must be classed as his youngest fan. 'A friend said: "Meet my three-year-old granddaughter, she prefers *Dad's Army* to *Postman Pat*."

'I couldn't believe my ears. An episode of *Dad's Army* had just been shown, during which the vicar had argued with Mainwaring over the use of the church hall office. The little girl stared up at me and said: "Whose desk is it, yours or Captain Mainwaring's?" So I thought, she not only watches it, but she really follows the plot!'

Born in London in 1931, Frank believes it was regular visits to the local cinema that fired his enthusiasm for becoming an actor. 'Neither of my parents was in the profession, so I was an oddity!' he laughs. 'Father, had retired early, so both parents were around while I was growing

up. I was always a keen cinemagoer and thought acting must be a glamorous life; I collected autographs and would hang around outside the stage door for ages waiting for the actors to come out of London theatres.'

Frank's first taste of acting was at a North London grammar school, where he completed his education. 'I wish I could have done more,' he says, 'because I'd always been interested in acting from a young age; as a small boy I remember dragooning all my friends into taking part in concerts and plays I'd written.'

Upon leaving school, he wanted to pursue his dream of becoming an actor. 'My father wasn't too keen. Earlier I tried persuading him to let me attend a children's drama school but he was adamant I should complete my education first. When I left school, having done Higher School Certificate, and was still determined to be an actor, my father gave me his full support.'

In 1951 Frank joined London's Gateway Theatre as a student ASM (assistant stage manager). Although he classed the job as a 'general dogsbody', it offered the chance of small parts in various productions, including Shakespeare, and a debut playing two parts: as a snail and an ant in *The Insect Play*.

His TV break was in 1952's *The Call Up*, a

dramatised documentary concerning conscripts going through national service training, followed three years later by *Those Who Dare,* about the building of the first open Borstal, with Frank playing the unlikely role of a Borstal boy. 'My first substantial TV part was during the same year in the play *The Queen Came By,* with Thora Hird.'

Frank, who's also made over 30 films, was first seen on the big screen in the 1956 British Lion production, *The Extra Day.* 'I played a cameraman, that was in the days when I had some hair!'

But he has no doubts as to the show that made his face familiar to TV viewers – *The Army Game.* He played several small parts, including a psychiatrist interviewing Bernard Bresslaw, before becoming a regular as Captain Pocket in some 70 episodes. 'I thought it was great being seen on TV. Sadly, my father didn't live long enough to see me attain 'real' success, but my mother saw me in *The Army Game* and was pleased I was doing well in my life.

'I had a wonderful time playing Captain Pocket, even though going out live was rather frightening. We did one show a week for 39 weeks of the year so it was a bit of a marathon.'

In 1957, Frank worked at The Palace Theatre, Watford, run by Jimmy and Gilda Perry. He had two of his own plays produced there and became chairman of the Patrons' Club, forming a strong friendship with Jimmy that was to reap benefits a decade later. 'I never dreamt that when I worked for him again it would be in one of the most successful shows ever created, *Dad's Army.'*

Frank didn't make his first appearance in *Dad's Army* until the 13th episode, *The Armoured Might Of Lance Corporal Jones.* 'Not only had I worked for Jimmy before, but I'd done a couple of episodes of *Hugh and I* for David Croft,' he says, 'so I didn't have to audition for the role. I was asked to go along for the one episode. It was a nice job to do but I thought it was only ever going to be a one-off engagement; then the vicar came back for more episodes, and the rest is history.'

As far as Frank is concerned, it's the strong characterisation that has made *Dad's Army* such a success. 'The characters themselves are funny and that's what appeals to people right across the age range, including children.'

During the filming of the series, Frank became close friends with Edward Sinclair, who played

A very young Frank Williams.

the verger. On screen the vicar was often waspish towards telltale Maurice Yeatman, a far cry from their close off-screen relationship. 'Teddy was a marvellous person and we got on so well together. Whenever it was time to travel up to Norfolk for location shooting, we'd always drive up together – it was great fun.

'Everything about the programme has been a joy. I was in the film, did several radio shows, and the stage show was an extremely happy 12 months.'

When he wasn't appearing in *Dad's Army*, Frank continued making the occasional film and appearing on stage, including three plays at The English Theatre, Vienna. 'I'm able to play straight roles over there because the audiences don't really know *Dad's Army*, so are able to take me seriously!

'Since *Dad's Army* finished, I haven't done as much TV work as I would have liked, but I'm

ROBERT MILL (b. London)
Role: Capt. Swan (episode 62); Army Capt. (episode 79)

After finishing national service, Robert began reading Classics at Oxford but left before gaining a degree. Moved between jobs for two years before joining RADA.

Became ASM at Margate, before spending time at Cambridge, Coventry and 18 months at Northampton in 1963. Theatre work is his great love (appeared in Tom Conti's 1991 production *Otherwise Engaged* at Windsor) but he's worked on TV in *Enemy of the State* in the 1960s, a version of Oscar Wilde's *The Canterville Ghost* with Bruce Forsyth, a vicar in *In Sickness and In Health* and *The First Churchills*. Has also made a few films.

He is also a busy member of the Equity Council.

grateful to Jimmy and David for giving me the chance to play the Bishop in *You Rang M'Lord?*

'I've been rather typecast in comedy roles. Serious parts sometimes seem few and far between, but that may be changing because I've just finished a long run in *A Midsummer Night's Dream*, directed by Jonathan Miller – I'll just have to wait and see.'

In the meantime, Frank, who's also a playwright, plans to pursue this side of his career. Over the past few years, there have been successful productions of four of his thrillers. 'But there are three other plays with a more serious content – I'd dearly love to see those produced.'

PERRY ON WILLIAMS
When I first thought of Dad's Army, even before the script was written, I knew we would need a vicar – and Frank's was the first name I wrote down. To me he was perfect casting as the Reverand Farthing, always slightly tetchy as he tried to come to terms with the platoon's invasion of his church hall.

The Stage Show

MAIN CAST
Arthur Lowe (Capt. Mainwaring)
John Le Mesurier (Sgt. Wilson)
Clive Dunn/Jack Haig (Lance Cpl. Jones)
Arnold Ridley (Pte. Godfrey)
Ian Lavender (Pte. Pike)
John Bardon (Pte. Walker)
Hamish Roughhead (Pte. Frazer).

SUPPORTING CAST
Joan Cooper (Miss Godfrey)
Pamela Cundell (Mrs Fox)
Janet Davies (Mrs Pike)
Other supporting members include:
Eric Longworth, Michael Bevis,
Norman MacLeod, Bernice Adams,
Debbie Blackett and Jeffrey Holland
(playing the Mad German Inventor).

PRODUCTION CREDITS
Written by Jimmy Perry and David Croft;
costumes by Mary Husband; directed by
David Croft and Jimmy Perry and staged
by Roger Redfarn.

In 1975 the responsibility of staging the
show was given to Roger Redfarn, whose
only link with Jimmy Perry and David
Croft up until then was that he shared

the same agent. Unsurprisingly, Roger
was excited at the prospect of working on
Dad's Army.

'Transferring the show from TV to stage
was a great challenge,' he says.
'Obviously the characters and their
relationships were already firmly
established, but I was responsible for how
the whole stage concept worked.

'I was also involved in casting some of
the supporting parts. I knew Jeffrey
Holland, for example, and cast him in a
small role. Straight away Jimmy and
David liked him so whenever any extra
bits cropped up, he got them.'

Well-known for his later success as
Spike in *Hi-De-Hi!*, Jeffrey was 'brassed
off' on the day he auditioned for the stage
production. 'I was working at Chichester
and enjoying myself, but couldn't stay on
because I'd only been booked for the first
two of four plays,' he recalls.

'I didn't want to go to the audition and
was in a terrible mood. Knowing I was
meeting Roger and Sheila O'Neill, the
choreographer, who I'd worked with many
times before, I didn't learn any lines.

'But then I had to meet David Croft and
Jimmy Perry, so when I was given a
script to read I found a version of the

song *Yes, We Have No Bananas* in the script for Walker to sing.

'In front of David and Jimmy, I started reading a few of Pikey's lines, to prove I could act, and then a few lines as a German inventor. And when they asked about singing, I did the song which they both enjoyed.

'When I'd finished they'd been laughing so much I asked whether they knew the song well, and was surprised when they claimed they'd never heard it before. I said: "What do you mean, you wrote it?" Jimmy replied: "We wrote it down, sent it to the typist and then completely forgot about it."'

Jeffrey was booked to play the German inventor as well as understudying Ian Lavender and John Bardon, who was playing Walker. One day at the Shaftesbury, he had to replace Ian Lavender for a matinee performance, a time he'll never forget.

'I went on with a scarf and funny hat and did all the scenes to the best of my ability. But because I wasn't Pikey, I never received a single laugh, except from the rest of the company behind me who were laughing up their sleeves.'

The show was essentially a series of sketches based on the TV series. Each segment was either an enlarged scene, shortened episode or new material specially written for the stage production. After six months in the West End, the

A scene from the theatre production.

Hanging out the washing on the Siegfried line.

show went out on tour around the country for a further six months. Audience numbers varied greatly between the venues. 'It seemed to be more of a south and east coast story than a north or west,' Roger explains.

One of the challenges Roger Redfarn faced was giving everybody in the cast a good crack of the whip. To make matters worse, when the show opened in Billingham it was too long. Scenes had to be cut to reduce the duration of the performance by 30 minutes, which meant there were even less lines to distribute.

But looking back, Roger believes the show was perfectly balanced and there's nothing he'd change. 'It was a very happy production to work on,' he says, 'and I'm sure everyone was pleased with what they did in it.'

One of his greatest pleasures was working with the cast. He has particular memories of his time with John Le

Mesurier. 'John often gave the impression that he wasn't quite with you. I remember during a technical rehearsal we concentrated on a scene with John and Arthur sitting in a sandbag truck.

'When we'd finished the truck was moved off stage and we prepared for the next scene involving John – the trouble was no one could find him! He was eventually discovered asleep in the sand truck.

'Another thing I remember about him was that he never liked being in the centre of the stage, preferring to linger around the edges,' says Roger. 'I eventually realised that this was because whenever he didn't have anything to do, he could lean against the side. He was certainly a very laid back actor.'

The Radio Series

MAIN CAST
Arthur Lowe (Capt. Mainwaring)
John Le Mesurier (Sgt. Wilson)
Clive Dunn (Lance Cpl. Jones)
John Laurie (Pte. Frazer)
Arnold Ridley (Pte. Godfrey)
Ian Lavender (Pte. Pike)
James Beck/Graham Stark/Larry Martyn
(Pte. Walker)

SUPPORTING CAST included:
Bill Pertwee (the ARP Warden),
Frank Williams (the Vicar),
Edward Sinclair (the Verger).
ALL EPISODES INTRODUCED BY JOHN SNAGGE.

PRODUCTION CREDITS
Adapted by Harold Snoad and Michael
Knowles; produced by John Dyas.

BROADCASTING DATES
Series One originally transmitted between
28.1.74 and 10.6.74.
Series Two originally transmitted between
11.2.75 and 24.6.75.
Series Three originally transmitted
between 16.3.76 and 7.9.76.
Christmas Special transmitted 24.12.74.

Harold Snoad, together with Michael Knowles, adapted the TV scripts for radio, not an easy job, as Michael recalls: 'It was difficult because the episodes were so visual. To translate them to sound terms meant quite a bit of rewriting, and doing that for 70 episodes was a hefty task.'

One example of an episode where the script couldn't simply be lifted from the TV version was *The Day The Balloon Went Up*, which features a scene where Mainwaring gets hoisted into the air by a stray barrage balloon the platoon are looking after.

On the screen it's only Mainwaring who's pulled up by the balloon – that had to change for the radio show. 'You can't have someone up in the air on their own for radio, so we rewrote the scene and Jones went up with him; that way the two characters could talk to each other.

'Some scenes were just too visual so we had no alternative but to go back to the drawing board and write a completely different scene. But Jimmy Perry and David Croft always saw the scripts before they were transmitted.'

Ian Lavender found the radio recording sessions exhausting.

The work schedule was often hectic with episodes occasionally recorded on the actors' day off from TV rehearsals. Ian Lavender also remembers a period when two episodes were recorded each day for a fortnight. 'We all felt brain dead by the time we'd finished,' recalls Ian Lavender. 'But they were great fun and worked well, even though, at times, they felt like a chore.'

Where are They Now?

It's 20 years since the last episode, *Never Too Old*, was originally screened, sufficient time for some actors who appeared in *Dad's Army* to have gone on to become household names. Others continue earning a steady income in character parts while a few have packed away the greasepaint and are enjoying a well-earned retirement. A few have left the profession altogether, while a saddening number have passed away since making their appearances in the classic sitcom.

But if you've ever wondered what some of the performers have been up to since making their contribution to the show's success, or whether he/she is still with us, here is an update on just a few of those not mentioned elsewhere.

BERNICE ADAMS, an ATS girl in *Number Engaged*, gave up acting in the early 1980s and works as manager of a theatrical company in Monte Carlo.
ROBERT ALDOUS, meanwhile, mainly works in theatre, although his sporadic forays into TV include appearances in *'Allo, 'Allo.*

Child actor **JOHN ASH** was the second and final person to play Jones' assistant Raymond. Now 42, it would appear he has left the acting scene. He was busy during the 1970s in shows like the BBC production of *Nicholas Nickleby*.
ROGER AVON, the doctor in *Branded*, is still busy working after 60 years in the profession, and ex-Post Office worker **RALPH BALL**, who appeared as a city gent in *Sons Of The Sea*, gave up acting in 1981 and now runs a theatrical agency with his wife.
MICHAEL BEVIS appeared in *Face On The Poster* as a consequence of being recruited for the stage show. Most of his time now is taken up writing and presenting music features for Radio 2.
DENNIS BLANCH, who attended drama school in the evenings while working at the London food markets, remains busy on TV. His appearances include: *Emmerdale*, *Heartbeat* and five years in *Strangers*.

JENNIFER BROWNE played a WAAF Sgt. in *The Day The Balloon Went Up*, and her appearance in 1969 marked the resumption of her acting career after living in Singapore for two years. Has since raised three children and three years ago decided to return again to acting. Mostly works in the theatre.

GEOFFREY CHATER, who popped up in *Round And Round Went The Great Big Wheel* as Colonel Pierce, had worked with David Croft years before at Hereford Rep. Has acted all his working life and made a recent appearance in *The Detectives*. PATRICK CONNOR played Irishman Shamus in *Absent Friends*. Started acting while working for the BBC as a studio manager. Eventually turned pro and joined Oldham Rep. After four decades in the business, during which he appeared in many TV shows including *The Professionals* and *The Persuaders*, he has semi-retired. DEIRDRE COSTELLO was the buffet attendant in *Mum's Army*. Since *Dad's Army* she has been seen in many productions, including a stint in *Grange Hill*, playing a parent, and *London's Burning*. A qualified teacher, Deirdre regularly works as a supply teacher in primary schools. Canadian-born BLAIN FAIRMAN, the US Sgt. in *My British Buddy*, is now a partner in a London conference and production company. As well as appearing in sitcoms like *The Fall and Rise of Reginald Perrin*, he has written and produced for the BBC. JEFFREY GARDINER, who made his TV debut as an interviewer in *The Larkins*, played Mr Wintergreen in *A Brush with the Law*. He has appeared in several Perry and/or Croft productions, including *Are You Being Served?* and *You Rang, M'Lord?* REX GARNER, Capt. Ashley-Jones in *Fallen Idol*, now lives in South Africa, while French-born ROBERT GILLESPIE, Charles Boyer in *A Soldier's Farewell*, has David Croft to thank for kicking-off his TV career as a Moroccan

police sergeant in *Hugh and I Spy*. Went on to appear in *Whatever Happened to the Likely Lads?* and five series of *Keep it in the Family*. Still busy acting. Playing the French General in *The Captain's Car*, JOHN HART DYKE had worked for Jimmy Perry at Watford. Began training as a chartered surveyor before joining a rep in Scotland. Most of his work since *Dad's Army* has been in the theatre, but seen on TV in *All Creatures Great and Small*, *Bergerac* and *Doctor Finlay*. ROSE HILL was Mrs Cole in *Uninvited Guests*. Now 80, she's been in the business six decades. An opera singer in her early life, Rose is best known as Fanny, the bedridden old lady, in *'Allo, 'Allo*. TONY HUGHES appeared as Mr Billings in *When Did You Last See Your Money?* Worked for a tobacco company before national service, after which he took up acting. His first TV work was presenting a kids' maths show. Now semi-retired, did a lot of commercial work after *Dad's Army*, including a long contract for Italian TV advertising *Lenor*.

SUZANNE KERCHISS was married to Ian Lavender when she appeared as Ivy in *My British Buddy*. Originally trained as a ballet dancer. Although she retains her Equity card, Suzanne now works as a nurse. JOHN LEESON was a soldier in *Sons Of The Sea*. After Dad's Army, he spent several years working as an announcer on the Forces network in Germany. As well as *Rings On Their Fingers*, John is best known as the voice behind K9 in *Dr Who* and for playing the original Bungo Bear in the children's show, *Rainbow*. Mainly does theatre and corporate videos now. Has also been a

Channel 4 announcer for ten years. **SUSAN MAJOLIER**, the nurse in *The Recruit,* worked as a dancer before switching to acting. Nowadays has a semi-regular role as Mason, the Chief Superintendent's secretary, in *The Bill.* Not actively seeking work, she spends most of her time with her children. The Scottish sergeant in *Number Engaged,* **STUART McGUGAN** worked as a journalist for six years before acting. A busy TV actor, he was Gunner Mackintosh in *It Ain't Half Hot, Mum* and spent nine years presenting *Play School.* Recent TV includes: *The Chief, Tutti Frutti* and *Hamish Macbeth.* **NORMAN MITCHELL,** who studied medicine at Sheffield University, has made over 2,000 TV appearances and 100 films during his long career. His credits include *All Creatures Great and Small* and *Yes, Minister.* **DONALD MORLEY** worked on *Going Straight* and *Open All Hours* after playing Glossip in *The Captain's Car.* Still working on TV, he also played Mollie Sugden's husband in Jeremy Lloyd and David Croft's *Grace and Favour.* **ROBIN PARKINSON** was Lieut. Wood, who dressed up as a gorilla in *Gorilla Warfare.* During a busy small screen career, he appeared in three series of *'Allo, 'Allo* playing Monsieur Leclerc. Has recently appeared in an episode of *Outside Edge* but works mainly in the theatre now. **DAVID ROSE** made his sole appearance in *Brain Versus Brawn.* He still acts and since *Dad's Army* credits include *Yes, Prime Minister* and *Howard's Way.* **KENNETH WATSON**, a RAF Officer in *The Day the Balloon Went Up*, is still busy on TV and was recently seen in *Wycliffe.* American-born **SERETTA WILSON,** a Wren in *Getting The Bird* who turned out to be Wilson's daughter, got the job thanks to John Le Mesurier. She had played his daughter in the series *A Class By Himself,* her TV debut. Other than a break to bring up her family, Seretta has continued acting and was seen recently in *The Bill.* She is also a qualified aerobics teacher.

   NIGEL HAWTHORNE went on to play Sir Humphrey Appleby in *Yes Minister* and *Yes, Prime Minister* and receive an Oscar nomination for *The Madness of King George.* **BILL TREACHER**, better known as Arthur Fowler in *EastEnders,* was seen briefly in *Menace From The Deep,* while **BARBARA WINDSOR** of *Carry On* and *EastEnders* fame made a guest appearance in the first series. **WENDY RICHARD** was seen in four episodes, usually playing Walker's girlfriend, before making her name in *Are You Being Served?* and *EastEnders.* **GEOFFREY HUGHES** made a cameo appearance in *Brain Versus Brawn* before playing Eddie Yeats in *Coronation Street.* More recently he has seen as Onslow in *Keeping Up Appearances.*

   Sadly, so many artists have died since *Dad's Army* finished its lengthy run. The roll call includes Tim Barrett, Michael Bilton, Amy Dalby, Roy Denton, Jay Denyer, J. G. Devlin, Arthur English, Chris Gannon, Fulton Mackay, Toby Perkins, Carl Jaffe, Natalie Kent, Sam Kydd, Barry Lineham, Pamela Wilson, Gladys Dawson, Alvar Lidell, Charles Morgan, Blake Butler, Tom Mennard, Andrew Carr and Charles Hill.

The Silent Soldiers

Peering over the shoulders of the platoon's front row was a band of nameless faces. They came in all shapes and sizes and with few, if any, lines of dialogue; they rarely appeared on the credits.

But although viewers never got to know their names, everyone expected to see a consistent batch of faces, partly for authenticity. Making up the line throughout the 80 TV episodes were many seasoned pros from all walks of the entertainment world.

During the life of the series, the personnel occasionally changed but a hard core became an inherent component in the platoon, as Jimmy Perry recalls. 'They were very important to the show. We were determined not just to have extras, but people who were performers in their own right. Some were retired and only too glad of the work, and all did a fine job.' David Croft adds: 'They were very loyal and enjoyed doing the show; most of them were very competent performers.'

Even though few were ever given a line to say, it was still important the actors knew their business. 'The fact that the person doesn't speak matters very little,' explains Jimmy.

'If they're not performers they don't look right. Professionals know what to do

Back row stalwart Vic Taylor.

and how to do it, they know how not to stand out – and that's important.'

Perhaps the most prominent member of the back row was Colin Bean (number 10 in the group shot overleaf) who was promoted to the front row later in the programme's run. He's proud to have

Alec Coleman.

Leslie Noyes.

been associated with *Dad's Army*.

'Nobody knew it was going to be such a long-runner. Jobs such as those in the back row of the platoon would not have really been of much interest to younger aspiring actors, but a godsend to older actors who may not have worked for some time, or who were making a career out of extra and walk-on work.'

The following pages offer some information about the more regular members.

Dad's Army

A group shot, featuring many of the Silent Soldiers.

1. RICHARD JACQUES, who now lives in Canada, trained at Bradford's Northern Theatre School before years of rep. Appeared in the episode *The Lion Has 'Phones* as Mr Cheesewright and two series as a platoon member before moving on. Now a director, writer and teacher of drama, he co-founded the English Theatre Company of Sweden and directed the stage version of Perry and Croft's *It Ain't Half Hot, Mum.*

2. ARTHUR McGUIRE served 20 years in the navy, during which time he had the opportunity to appear as an extra in a few films including *A Matter of Life and Death,* for which he was paid £3 a day, and *The Baby and the Battleship.* When he joined civvy street he turned to walk-on work and was regularly employed in shows like *The Saint* and *The Persuaders.* He also did commercials. He died of a heart attack in 1987, aged 61. Arthur appeared in a handful of early episodes prior to 1970.

3. HUGH CECIL, who stayed with the platoon throughout its life, was a professional magician after the war. Still a well-known Punch and Judy man, Hugh performed his show in Tommy Steele's *Half a Sixpence* and *The Bill.* His first work was an extra in *Z Cars.* Bald-headed Hugh, who's still busy, is also in demand for photographic modelling. Among Hugh's recent work is an appearance in a Spice Girls video and the BBC production *Real Women,* playing the bride's grandfather.

including *The Two Ronnies* and *Are You Being Served?* playing Arthur English's assistant. He died in 1984.

6. DAVID SEAFORTH, who gave up an electrical engineering apprenticeship, was 20 when he appeared in the first series. It was planned he would become a platoon regular, but other work commitments prevented him furthering the role. An ex-graduate of *Opportunity Knocks*, David has made occasional TV appearances, including two parts in *Crimewatch*. Nowadays he earns his living mainly in hotel cabaret, working this summer in Rhodes.

7. DESMOND CULLUM-JONES, born in America, was a sales rep before turning to acting in his late twenties. Worked hard in small parts in shows including *Z Cars*, *Dixon of Dock Green* and *Father, Dear Father*. The money he earned was directed into his letting business. Also ran a fashion photo agency in London. He is financially independent due to property ownership, and although he no longer does walk-ons he is still active in the business. Recently seen as a magistrate in the television dramatisation of one of Catherine Cookson's novels.

8. VERNON DRAKE was a well-known music hall and variety performer. For 25 years he was part of the successful double act, Connor and Drake. During the Great War, he served with the Royal Flying Corp. His career gradually moved into showbiz, and he has appeared in many successful musical comedies. He died in 1987, aged 90.

4. FRANK GODFREY was an old pro who'd been a performer all his life before moving into theatre management including the Palace Theatre, Watford.

5. JIMMY MAC started his career in a circus aged 12. Worked as a boy entertainer in Blackpool before later managing his own summer shows and pantomimes. A famous panto dame, he played many years at the Theatre Royal, Bath. Appeared in numerous TV shows

9. RICHARD KITTERIDGE In his early twenties when he appeared, Richard was seen in a number of early episodes. A six-episode run at the beginning of Season Three included *Battle School* and *The Lion Has 'Phones*. He was scheduled to become a regular but other work stopped this happening. Richard gave up an apprenticeship in motor mechanics to attend the London Academy of Modelling. Joining Equity in 1967, he mixed photographic work with walk-on parts on TV. His first job was as a TV soldier in a BBC play. After *Dad's Army* he carried on with mainly photographic work until quitting the profession and buying a petrol station in 1986. He subsequently ran a business selling go-kart parts. Nowadays, he works for the local council while minicabbing during the evening.

The following also served in the back row:

ROGER BOURNE served in the Royal Artillery Company with Jimmy Perry. He was part of the double-act Bourne and Barbara. Did a lot of walk-ons and appeared in small parts on TV and in films. Retired in 1980 but shortly after suffered a nervous breakdown. Ill health affected him until his death in early 1997.

FREDDIE WHITE was a farmer before the Second World War and became involved in the hotel industry afterwards. A keen amateur actor, he developed his thespian interests after a heart attack forced his retirement from the hotel trade. Only ever appeared on TV in walk-ons due to health restrictions. He died in 1993.

GEORGE HANCOCK, who died in 1992, was a retired opera singer who sang all over the world. A blacksmith in the coal mines after leaving school, he later graduated from the Royal College of Music. Sang professionally until after the war. Turned to TV work as he got older, doing a lot of small part work including two episodes of *Steptoe and Son*. Got his name on the credits once as Private Hancock in *The Godiva Affair*.

EVAN ROSS joined the squad in 1972 after the death of Vic Taylor. After winning a scholarship to the Royal Academy of Music he became an opera singer before moving into acting with extra work. Was a regular on *Crackerjack* as a policeman in comedy sketches. Now a freelance singer.

MICHAEL MOORE became a well-known radio star thanks to *Ignorance is Bliss*. Also worked in theatre and journalism.

FREDDIE WILES worked in a confectionery factory before becoming a sales rep for an asphalt company either side of the war. He'd always fancied acting, so upon retiring from industry he registered with an agency and started appearing as an extra on TV. Joined *Dad's Army* when a fellow platoon member left through illness. During the series he once doubled up as Clive Dunn and drove Jones' van in an episode. His last job was in a chocolate cake commercial in Rome. He died in 1983, aged 78.

HUGH HASTINGS, born in Australia, now 80, is a brilliant pianist, who wrote the highly successful *Seagulls Over Sorrento.* Was in the platoon until 1972 when he left to appear in a play. Spent eight years with the Young Vic Company, touring Mexico, USA and Australia. Had a small part and a screenplay credit in the 1950s' film, *The Gift Horse.* In the late 1980s he played piano in a restaurant. He is presently writing a novel.

LESLIE NOYES, originally a tap dancer, worked as a stooge for Arthur Haynes. Although he worked in America for a while as a dancer, his career was dominated by variety. He died in 1976 from cancer.

VIC TAYLOR worked as a builder's labourer after the war before taking up stunt work in his early twenties. Later turned to modelling, making a decent living from commercials and mail order catalogue work. His face appeared on boxes of Saxo stuffing for years. He was in his thirties when he moved into extra work on TV, but always continued as a model. Vic was a regular member of the platoon until his death from cancer in 1972. He was 48.

ALEC COLEMAN, an expert in military traditions, advised George Ward in respect of the costumes before the series began. As a member of the platoon, he appeared in the first two series before other commitments saw him leave. After the war he turned to acting full-time, appearing in theatre and TV, including *Compact, The Wednesday Play* and *The Tommy Cooper Show.* As a sideline, he worked as a London cabby. During the 1970s he moved to Manchester and worked in the ceremonial department at Manchester Town Hall while doing the occasional acting job for Granada in shows like *Country Matters.*

PETER WHITAKER a regular in the first series, trained as a singer at London's College of Music. For many years he worked in theatre, while turning to walk-ons and commercials as fill in work. Among his TV appearances was an episode of *Upstairs, Downstairs.* Now 76, Peter has retired. He turned down the chance of appearing more often as a platoon member.

WILLIAM GOSSLING appeared throughout the sixth season. After working in an engineer's office for most of his career he was made redundant in his 50s. Unsure what to do next, his actress wife persuaded him to take up walk-on work. Thanks to fellow platoon member George Hancock, Williams joined *Dad's Army.*

He was kept busy in various shows, including *The Tommy Cooper Show* any many TV productions of Shakespeare. Also did film work. He was in demand until illness stopped him working. William died in 1981, aged 69.

Before You Fall out

So it's time to close. One of the most difficult decisions when writing a book, particularly when it's about one of your favourite TV shows, is deciding when to stop. Usually the decision is made for you once you check the word count, but frustration is always rife because you usually feel there is much more that should be written. Alas, one has to be practical. Within the book I've concentrated on areas I believe most fans would want to know about concerning this perennial favourite.

The continuing success of *Dad's Army* is remarkable; there is surely nothing to match it in the annals of British comedy. Nearly 30 years old, Perry and Croft's gem is still adored by millions; and what is reassuring for its long-term future is that its appeal reaches out and earns the allegiance of new fans, many of whom seem hardly out of nappies! I've been fortunate enough to experience this firsthand: when a recent screening of an episode induced my six-year-old niece, Samantha, and nine-year-old nephew, Christopher, into singing the words of the signature tune, I could hardly believe it. What other TV programme can lay claim to such never-ending appeal?

This book has been a joy to write, not just because it's meant revisiting all the episodes again, but it has afforded me the opportunity to meet and speak with many of the people who brought this legend to life, most notably, of course, its creators Jimmy Perry and David Croft.

I hope you find this book not just interesting but informative as well. One of the show's strengths was the calibre of its characterisations, even down to the one-line cameo appearances. Within these pages I've tried to focus on as many of the 200-plus actors who appeared in the series as possible. Space has prevented me including as much biographical information as I would have liked. For the smaller profiles featured I have picked characters who are particular favourites of mine, regardless of how many episodes they appeared in. Others have been selected because of the number of appearances they made during the programme's life. I just hope your personal favourites are included.

If you would like more information about *Dad's Army* then why not join the appreciation society? For details, write to: Jack Wheeler, Dad's Army Appreciation Society, 8 Sinodun Road, Wallingford, Oxfordshire OX10 8AA.

**Richard Webber,
Clevedon, 1997**